This is R J Rossiter's first attempt at writing a book. Being a first-time writer, he had to overcome his fear of writing, as he suffers from dyslexia and ADD. R J Rossiter wrote this book during the most challenging period of his life. It gave him an escape and an avenue to express his overactive imagination. This whole experience has been an enjoyment and a really big help with overcoming his inability to read and write and in the way it helped to build his confidence.

This book is dedicated to me and to everyone out there who has ever doubted themselves. This book is my way for finally letting go of my issues, my past, and realising that I've got a gift and I'm not afraid of it.

R J Rossiter

THE FIVE REALMS OF THE EMERALD KINGDOM

The Missing General

AUSTIN MACAULEY PUBLISHERS™

LONDON • CAMBRIDGE • NEW YORK • SHARJAH

A CIP catalogue record for this title is available from the British Library.

ISBN 9781528984362 (Paperback)
ISBN 9781528984379 (ePub e-book)

www.austinmacauley.com

First Published 2022
Austin Macauley Publishers Ltd®
1 Canada Square
Canary Wharf
London
E14 5AA

I would like to say to both of my gorgeous daughters that I can't thank you enough for being not only my kids but for being my best friends.

Also, a big thank you to everyone that has helped me in some way including the #squad.

Chapter 1

Home

I wasn't really awake; my eyes were closed and my brain wasn't working as I laid there. I could hear the birds from outside the window and felt the sun on my face. As it came through, its warmth was comforting to me as it always was. I wanted to move. I needed to move but I just kept laying there in my half awaken state. I didn't really know if I were alive or if I was dreaming. What feel like years later, I finally got up walked over and looked out the window. I saw what I always saw: green, an Ocean of greenery. In fact, the trees and the meadow which lead down to the river; my little house was on the top of a small hill on the edge of the forest. It's the most amazing place in the world or so I seem to think. I've seen most of the world and didn't intend to see any more of it, so I stubbornly believe I have everything I need here to live my simple life in my little house and with my animals plus the forest and the river both give me everything I need to survive here on my own.

There's a town a few miles downriver and once a month or so when it's market day, I get in my boat and go shopping. It's the absolute worst morning of my life but as no one knows who I am, it's easy to get in and get it done before they're sticking their noises in your business and them wanted this that or the other "no thank you".

Now as much as I'm a grumpy old man with no friends, I'm not actually that old. At the grand age of 70, I'm still a very young man and for the last few years, I lived with my horse, the general, a few chickens and the biggest pig you have ever seen and I've lived it all by myself in the middle of nowhere and I love it. Besides that, the forest is where the real goods are. There I can hunt rabbits, pigeons and once a year a deer. In between that, the river full of fish plus I have my little garden on the side of my house. All in all, it's a good life or so I think.

Today was a special day and one I've been looked forward to. Now you remember the deer I mentioned. Well, today is hunting day. It's late summer and I'm going to hunt myself a deer but not just any deer. No, I'm not some common hunter who slaughters for the sake of it. Oh no. This particular deer is old and as I spotted a few weeks back, it has a bad leg so not only am I doing him a favour, it will feed and clothe me for months and as winter is coming, a new deer skin will make my bed very warm indeed. I packed my bag, picked up my bow and head out the door. It's going to be a long day. It was a warm summer's morning, as I headed over to the barn to check on the general eating as usual. 'I see, old friend,' I said to him. No reply. He just gives me the oh you not taking me out again look and ignores me. Then after I've tripped over the chickens for the tenth time, I'm off out the door and down the path to the boat house. I make my way through the meadow which is always full of flowers this time of year. Then after a few minutes, I'm off down the river towards the coast. I'm not actually going all the way out to the open water for the bay as

I would have to go through our capital and beyond and that's not a place I wanted to go back to any time soon. Too many bad memories for my liking plus that's where they will be waiting of the poor innocent people to fall into their trap. The pirates won't silly or so they thought but I knew only too well what they were like. I go down river for a few miles. I peel off down a small waterway to the left a few metres down these, an old tree blocking the way. It's the perfect place to hide my boat. The next bit is the hardest as it's all on foot and uphill but after some time, I finally reach the end of the path. By then, I'm sweating hot and out of breath but as I see it for the first time, I know it was worth it. The grasslands of the seven hills is my hunting spot for the afternoon. It's a place I know very well. It's full of big trees, lovely flowers and the fresh air. It's a great place to just sit and relax but I'm not here to relax. I'm here to hunt deer. After what seem like some hours of sitting in the afternoon sun, I finally spot the deer that I wanted. I had to wait a little bit longer but then after the best shot of my life I managed to get my price. It takes me a couple of hours to get it to the boat but then I was off home once more and once I got there, I got the deer hung up in my larder then back into the house. Now it was time for food, wine and my chair which was right in front of the fire a lovely evening after a very long day, but it's all been worth it.

The next few days, I spend at home keeping myself busy doing all the little things that I need to do. It's not long before the days turn into weeks and the green of summer turns into the brown of autumn. The air starts to cool and the edges of the river start to freeze over. All the animals are all well covered and warm in the barn and my Larder is well stocked with the goods from my summer hunts. I still have half the deer, rabbits and more to keep me going for a good while yet but unfortunately, the wine has gone so a very uncomfortable trip to market has to be made at some point and as the boat froze in the boat house, I'll be dragging my very grumpy horse out into the cold. *That's not going to end well,* I thought to myself. When market day came, I got everything ready. Me and the general left first thing in the morning. The trail through the Forster was long, straight and boring but as it's well covered, it's not too cold and we make good time to the market. Once there, I left the general in the stable and headed around to the market place. It was surprisingly busy and full of people which is not great and really not what I was expecting. There was a sense of happiness and celebration in the air. Not living in the town, I had no idea what all the fuss was about or indeed what was going on. As I wandered through the market, I kept hearing people say "when is he coming" or if he would stay long. I had no idea what was going on so when I got to the winery, I had to ask what was all the fuss about. The merchant looked at me laughed and said how do you not know who or what going on today and called me a fool, "fool" "what" how very dear of you, I wanted to say to him.

'Do you really know who this fool is? No, I bet you don't.' I've never been so offended in my life but the truth was, I didn't know and he didn't know who I was and I didn't want him knowing either and honestly, I didn't care. I packed up my goods and made my way back to the stables.

As I made my way back, I stopped dead in my tracks. A sense…a sound…something that I never thought I'd feel again. Then the flash of darkness from above and the sound of his wings. I know it only too well. I hurried back to the stables.

I had to get the general and get out of there. I could hear it as I loaded up my horse. We rushed out of the stables. Then as I approached the town walls and the road, our way was blocked by the cheering crowd and I had to stop. Then the thud as he landed. I raised my head and saw him for the first time in a very long time. The king of all the magical creatures. The winter sun was shining off of him. He looked as big and as magnificent as he always did but there was something different this time. I ducked back and moved into the side street. I didn't want him seeing me here. As I looked back, I could see that for the first time in my life, he wasn't alone. There were two of them and what a sight it was. I had to find out what was going on but then I couldn't risk him seeing me or finding me again and for everyone else knowing who I really was but how to get out of there, the town was full and the gates were closed. Living a life on my own, I knew how to keep myself to myself. Staying hidden was the only way out of this. So, I made my way back to the stable. No one would even notice this old fool walking away from all the fuss that was going on in the town and a fuss it was. What was really going on? And why was he even there? And why was there two of them? Too many questions for my liking, question mean answers both I don't want to know or get involved in that life. Those people and those problems were over for me now. I didn't want it or need it.

Waking the next morning was not nice. Sleeping in the hay in a stable full of horses was not ideal and the smell was ridiculous but as all was quiet, me and the general made our way out of town and for home. After a while, we were out and into the woods. It was a big relief knowing home wasn't far away but my mind was now troubled with what I'd seen. Why would he be there? And who was his friend? Too many questions and unfortunately, my relief wasn't to last long. The general heard it first then me. The sounds of his wings again. We were being followed, chased. Even the general didn't need telling. Twice with a thud of hoof, he was alive again and thundering off down the path. Like myself, he may have looked old but he had a spring in his step and a few tracks to match. After a few miles, it seems like we had lost him. As we arrived back into the meadow, seeing home again was the best feeling. I always got it every time I came back home from the market, but this time it was definitely better. There had been too much excitement for my liking. As we went up the path and home became even closer, I heard a bang and felt a swipe of air. I knew what it was. He must have seen me and now he had found me. I didn't get a chance to look around. With a swipe of tail, he knocked me clear off my horse and out cold.

Again, as I woke, I could feel the sun on my face. It was always a comforting feeling but not this time. I had no idea where I was or how long I had been out for. As I came around, I didn't feel right. Something or someone was there with me. I couldn't be sure but I knew who it was. The sound of him breathing…and just his breathing gave it away. Then the voice that came booming out of the shadows. 'Hello, my old friend,' he said and then I saw him standing there, the blue mystic, seven feet tall and a thousand pounds of hair, looking straight at me with that stupid look on his face. I smiled and said, 'Hello yourself,' while rubbing my sore head.

'Did he really have to hit me that hard?' I said, getting up from the bed. No answer. Just another stupid look then an answer.

'Ask him yourself. Come on, he's waiting for you.' With that, he turned and left. I washed my face from the bowl of water on the side, got dressed and went outside to the courtyard. Once outside, I was greeted to a sight I hadn't seen for nearly 20 years. She was as beautiful as I had remembered her to be. The silver witch in all her glory. Her white dress was magnificent and I couldn't do anything other than stand there and look at her smiling though as she walked over and slapped me in the face. The smile didn't last very long and being called an old fool again wasn't very fun either. She walked off and the monkey followed. Oh sorry, I forgot to mention old Blue was a 7ft tall Mountain gorilla and one of the members of the earth council. The council of which there are four, two from the human world and two from the magical. They protect all the people the animals and the earth itself. I wasn't a member but I was a supporter to the council but I still didn't know what they wanted with me. There were hundreds of wizards and witches in our world both for the dark and the light side of magic but anyway, I followed on. I didn't really have a choice as I still didn't really know where I was. I had never seen this place before. After a few minutes, I walked into a massive hall and in front of me was Largo, the dragon, king of all the magical creatures and the oldest member of the council. He looked at me and started laughing.

'Well, my boy,' he said.

'Hello, Largo. Long time.'

'Yes, boy, it is and why may I ask have you been hindering away in the outreach lands of nowhere living like a commoner?' Unfortunately, as amazing as he was, he was also a pain in the neck and probably right.

'None of your business,' I said, 'Largo, but you of all people should know exactly why now may I ask what it is you want with me. What do any of you want with me?'

'Witch, tell him.'

Boom, that voice again; the monkey was never quiet.

'Sit down,' she said. I hadn't been this close to her in so long. I felt a bit nervous and excited all at once. 'You are a supporter to this council?'

'Yes,' I replied.

'You are sworn by a code as and when it's needed, yes?'

'Yes, I know all of that but why me? There's a thousand other people who are good and supportive to you all more powerful and still connected in that world. I haven't seen you in 20 years, why me? Why now?' I said a little too angrily.

'It's because you've been gone so long that we need you. Now you know the code and the law and how this world works but you've not been connected so that should give you an advantage.'

'Advantage to what?' I asked.

'Listen, boy,' Largo said, 'while you've been off living a sad, lonely life, some of us still had a job to do. The fight has never been over for us. Now haven't you noticed something?' I took a long look at him at the witch and all around the room.

'Yeah, there's something missing, all right? Or actually someone.'

Four members of the council. There are and only four. It doesn't matter why or where they meet but if the council has a meeting, all members must be there so why wasn't there four. Again, too many questions for my liking and they will need answering. My little house, the general; it all seem so far away now. My life was changing and I didn't like it. I could feel myself getting pulled into something that I couldn't control. What was I getting in to here? I didn't want to ask as I turned around and felt myself saying, 'Largo, where is the golden master?'

A few minutes of nothing as they all looked at me, then the witch spoke to me. 'We don't know,' she said in her calm soft voice. I just stood there thinking. Now, the council members live in different parts of the kingdoms, lead different lives and so on but to not know where one of the earth council members was a bit extreme. This really wasn't going well but I had to ask one more question after that. 'Where's the leopard?'

Again, I got nothing before Blue said, 'We don't know that either.'

After the meeting with the council, I was escorted back to the room. I had woken up in early. I felt a bit trapped like a prisoner almost. Being away from home wasn't a nice feeling especially with all these questions I had. I was getting pulled into something I didn't want or like. After a few minutes of walking around the room thinking to myself, the door opened and the witch walked in. 'Hello,' she said with that beautiful voice and with that amazing smile of hers. Unfortunately, it was met by me and the very angry and confused looked I had on my face.

'Why me? Why now? And why has no one been looked for that leopard? And why two dragons?'

'Okay, okay,' she said, 'calm down. I know this is hard for you to take it all in.'

'Hard,' I snapped, 'why are you even talking to me; you nearly—'

'No,' she snapped back. 'That's not important. Not here not now. There are bigger things going on. I asked Largo to find you. You are the only one we trust enough. The only one who's good enough and who will not attract too must attention to them self.'

'I'm not that person anymore,' I replied, 'and we since when did Largo even really know or care for me?'

'WE?' boom that voice again, as Blue walked in.

'Me and the witch know you, trust you. We need your help now to find the master or at least know what happens to him if the darkness has started to go after council members again and yes even be ready for war. We need to know. Our friends our family all need to know. You know enough about this and what happened beforehand.'

'You don't need us to tell you what this means, my friend.' Silence had fallen in the room. It was getting a bit too much. I hadn't seen these people for so long and what they were asking for me was just too much. Blue looked at me with that big hairy gorilla head for a minute before he left. The witch looked at me as well maybe in not such a good way. This time, my old life really had caught up with me and I didn't like it one bit.

'Think about it, please,' she said. 'We won't force you into this,' she said. 'I know why you left us, left me and I will never blame you for what happened back then. I just really wish you hadn't done it.' I couldn't help but feel guilty. I knew exactly what she meant and after all this time, I still had the same feeling inside. As she went to leave, I reached out for her.

'Please one more question,' I said, as I held her arm.

'What?' she replied.

'Where am I?' She gave me that smile again.

'Follow me.'

We walked through a maze of hallways, tunnels and more rooms until she stopped at a doorway. She opened it up and held me by the hand. She led me up a stairway till we reached the top. Then as she opened enough door, bright sunlight hit me. We went outside, as she looked at me.

'I know how much you love the warmth of the sunshine,' she said and it was warm. I closed my eyes. The feeling of home rushed over me and straight away, I felt better as I could feel the sun on my face. I opened my eyes and laid out in front of us were hills and grasslands. The odd tree here and there. It really was a wonderful sight.

'But where I am?' I asked her.

'The northern mountains ranges are behind us and go from here in the west all the way to Blue's home in the east,' she said. 'The foot hills and grasslands for the Middle Kingdoms are stretched out in front of us and you live over that way,' she said, as she pointed to the left.

Wow, I thought to myself. 'But how do you know where I live?' I asked. She smiled at me.

'Just because you'd been gone doesn't mean you've been forgotten about,' she added smiling, 'plus that's where Largo said he found you.'

'Oh, I see and there's me thinking you knew where I was this whole time,' I said smiling back at her.

'I know I've not seen you in a very long time but I have missed you,' she said.

'Oh, did you really?' I said teasing her. She turned around with her arms open.

'This is Thorberg,' she said, 'and this is my home. In the morning, we'll take you back to your home. She walked back over to me taking my hand. You and only you can choose to help us. Me or Blue won't force you into this so please think long and hard about what we're asking of you.' And with that, she kissed me before leaving me with only the sunshine as comfort and a mindful of troubled thoughts.

Chapter 2

The Council, V the Darkness

The golden master was a human man. He was a great wizard and at 150 years old, a very wise man. He believed in the spirits and had a very powerful connection to both the human and magical worlds. He lived in a very old temple in the middle of the jungle to the east. The jungle itself went from the tropical sea in the south right up to where Blue lived in the cloud covered forest of the northern mountains. He believed in and cared for all that surrounded him, not only the different creatures but for the jungle itself. It had saved him in the past and now it was his turn to repay that favour, the temple was a place for all, full of birds and you would find a deer, warthog or two in the morning mists. It was also a place for the monkeys to be. They were a very common sight there because it was easy picking for them but the master didn't mean any of that. The leopard, Nina, who was more like the master's bodyguard; well, she did mind that the monkeys were a permeant torment to her. She had lived with the master in their jungle home for a very long time. The master and she grew up together and as much as she wanted to eat them, she thought better of it. Then there was Mimi, the python, or as I call her the man-eater. Though I had only been to the temple once before and seen her very briefly, she still scared me. She was the biggest snake I had ever seen. But she wasn't just the master's pet, she was the temple guard. The master knew he never had to worry about unwanted newcomers with her around. The master was also a protector to anyone and everyone, human or animal alike, who lived in the region. The jungle wasn't the nicest place for most. It was hot and it had its dangerous parts but the master had lived in it for so long now that he was very comfortable there. So how the hell did he manage to just disappear like that? The jungle was a big place, yes! And as a council member, he was responsible for a great many things and yes, he was well travelled. Everyone knew that but he never went anywhere without that leopard who you really wouldn't want to mess with, but as I said to the witch where was she? Anyway, the fact that no one had seen either of them was not a good thing. It just meant more questions and definitely not enough answer.

The council members all had prices on them and they all knew it. The dark side of the world had its dangers. There were warlords and dark witches and wizards not to mention the pirates who would rob anyone out on the waterways and the bandit causing nothing but trouble on land. They all wanted the council out of the way, so they could take control of the earth and the lands and the power that it came with. The earth for the must was a peaceful place and the council kept it that way. The darkness just keeps to the shadows and didn't really do too much damage. Well, that what I believe. If there wasn't that protection, there and they did start to take over the earth. War, green, money would all take over everything and that wasn't a very nice image. The warlords would kill and slaughter for the money and destroy anyone for the power and the control of it all.

Largo, the dragon king, was 1000 years old. He had been on the council for such a long time and he had been at war with the darkness for even longer than that. I had known him before my simple life. The same as he knew. The real me from before I went off to live on my own and he was part of that very reason. But not very many people did know him or where he came from or indeed where he actually lived or if he even had a home or a family because of his age, he had been battling both the human and the magical sides of the darkness for such a long time. He did whatever he could to keep the light and the world safe, to protect the people and to keep the earth at peace. He knew only too well of the danger he and the other council member faced. He may have been a mighty dragon but he was covered in the scars from the many battles he had been in and there was only a handful of dragons left in the world. Which is why I was so shocked to see two of them in one place together in the little market town the day he found me. But dragons although they were big and powerful, they weren't the only creatures in our world that were magical; many of them could talk like Blue and Largo.

Talking of the Blue mystic, he was a seven feet tall talking gorilla and my friend. I wasn't sure how old Blue was and I had never thought to ask him. He had been my friend for 50 years and he was also a wizard. He lived in the cloud-covered forests of the northern mountains and protected it just as the master did in the south. He had been on the council since before I was a supporter. He lived in a little village in fact that was high up in the treetops. To the common eye, you would never notice it but if like me you knew where to look, you could spot it a mile away. The village was a group of huts about 20 or so high up and all linked by bridges. Blue and his gorilla family lived with a group of humans along with the birds, insects and the odd squirrel. The forest was full of all sorts though with the likes of the bears, elephant and small cats on the ground plus other moneys in the trees. Together the strange looking group all lived, worked and cared for each other. They made their part of the forest a very peaceful place but unfortunately, there was always a danger of poachers hunting in the forest and not just for the animals but also for the people. They could sell them to the pirates for slaves and if they could get their hands on a magical creature, that would be even more money in that but that if they could find one. Now don't get me wrong, I hunted one deer a year to feed myself never on the scale. They were doing it but Blue and his forest family were smart and they would do whatever they could to stop it and to protect their part of their forest homeland. Tracking the poachers was easy. They weren't very quiet or clever. They would crash though the forest leaving all their rubbish behind so knowing where they were and what they were doing was easy for the gorillas. Now not all the gorillas could talk like Blue could but they could all understand the humans and believe me the gorillas and the humans they lived with didn't like them one bit. In between all of that, life was good. In the north, there were no big towns or settlements and Blue was comfortable in the treetops. It was safe away from the rest of the world. It was a place I know only too well and love visiting. We weren't in the treetops though we had been at a meeting in a place I had never been to before talking about a missing wizard and not just any wizard. Either a council member, I still didn't know exactly where I was or how far away from home I was, but I did know that the questions were getting more and more and I started to wonder if I would see my home any time soon.

The last member of the council and of course my favourite was the sliver witch. She was a human woman and the newest member to the council. She was a very beautiful, young lady and at 70 years old, she was the same age as me. I had known her before she was on the council. She was slim and very fit with her long blonde hair and she always looked so beautiful in her white dress and had a smile to match that would always melt my heart every time she looked at me. She like her mother and grandmother before that were not only witches but they were all members of the council at some point. Her family had very strong connections to the earth, the council and to the light of the world. She was once my…friend but unfortunately, a friend I hadn't seen for a very long time. There were only a few who knew her real name. Sahara, the sliver witch. She lived in a secret world deep inside a mountain somewhere in the northwest and no one, not even me in till today, knew where it was. Out of the four, she lived the most secretive of lives. Her mother taught her that even with her power, she could never afford to be too careful. Her mother sadly gave her live to save Largo from the darkness and almost certain death. It's a day that I will never forget and one I've been running away from for far too long, but you couldn't miss Sahara when she went out travelling like all the council member knew they had to do. Her white carriage was pulled by a pack of husky dogs who could run at great speed and travel great distance and she was always escorted by four bodyguards. Powerful she may have been but not stupid. Another thing her mother taught her and lot more than that to like her magic, the earth and the council everything about the good the bad and unfortunately the very ugly in our world.

The council wasn't just made up of four members, it was much bigger than that. I was one of hundreds of supporters from people that I knew and had none and from all walkers of life all from the human, animal and magical parts of this world, we were all part of a code "as and when its needed" to live and to protect. From the king in the capital down to the smallest mice out in the grasslands of the middle kingdom. Once you were a part of it, then there was no going back from it, and now they were asking me. I knew that this wasn't something I could just ignore even if Sahara did say they wouldn't force me into doing it. I know it was my duty to act and to do what they wanted but how and where to even start my mind was trouble from all the questions I had, but I knew I had failed her once before even if I had never turned my back on the code. It all felt like the same thing but I knew I wasn't ready for what was coming next.

The council had four members and hundreds of supporters. They all helped protect the earth and keep its people safe from the darkness and have done for over a century. There had been many battles between the lords and their armies both good and bad, between the witches and wizards again both from the light and dark side of magic. I for one have lost many friends and even my king to the darkness and its followers, but the darkness wasn't just one evil person like a witch or wizard. It wasn't a group like the pirates or the warlords and their armies. It was everything bad in the world both from the human and magical worlds alike. The darkness didn't even really have any order or a leader like the council as such. Yes, it had a few powerful people who were wise but not in a good way. Largo had many battles with the darkness, the ultimate battle between good and evil. There were also many other blood-hungry warlords, like Soren Kane; who was a very big and nasty man. Indeed, he had nothing but greed in his heart and along with his army to call upon but there were all out for them self which is why you never had two parts working together. They would fight each other just as much as they would fight against the light. They were all too selfish to see that they could gain much more by working and building something together than they ever could on their own. That was great for us and we knew it. We even tried to use that against them whenever we could. The human man like the warlords didn't have any honour and would just do whatever they wanted to take control and to fight over the power that would come with it. This was what made the darkness what it was, but the magic ones had a bit more respect for each other than that. When they fought, it wasn't to kill. It was to shame the other one and to prove how powerful they were. That didn't always go to plan as you can imagine. There is one who seems different. Her name is Sasha. She was one of many witches who served the darkness but she was a bit smarted than most. She was a beautiful woman who had black hair and dressed all in black. Like the master, she too had a power connection to the magic of the world like most but unfortunately, to the dark magic, she had a problem with control, and a bad temper to match and was very nasty with it. She wasn't one to be messed with and any man that did was always turned into something, well, horrible. Her father was a wizard, a good one at that, but he was killed by a gang of robbers when she was just a young girl. Some years later, she found those who did it and went after them and once she had found them, she lost any control she did have and turned them all to stone. That was the first time she used black magic and she has never stopped. She now lives in an old castle in the north of the middle kingdom and in the courtyard of that very castle are the statues of those very men. Alongside some very weird pets, she has ducks, frogs a lot of pigeons, a dog, a fat old pig and an old donkey all rumoured to be the man that had tried to cross her in the past. I myself had fought with her once a long time ago in my previous life. I had a lucky escape that time.

The black shadows weren't just a couple of lightweight horsemen. They were the worst of what the darkness had to offer. Hundreds of men who could all handle themselves in a fight and they were all growing by the day. Kane was drawing more for them to his army. The shadows also had more than just a larger group of man. They had a pack of lions and wolves, not to mention the bear called Whistleroot. They could all be called upon whenever they were needed and were always hungry for anyone who got in their way. The whole group travelled around the kingdoms robbing and causing as much damage as they could hunting anyone who got in their way and all for a profit and greed. The local lords and their men weren't really a match but they did what they could to keep them moving from place to place. But this time now, Sasha was involved. It all seemed a lot more dangerous. They seemed more organised and it's as if they had a purpose now. None of it was good. If war was coming, then they're already in front and ready for a fight that we didn't even know was coming.

Whistleroot, the bear, was the biggest and scariest thing you had ever seen in your life. He wasn't just big; he was massive and had a temper to match. We had a history. Whistleroot was the very bear from my past. I didn't even know he was still alive. He was taller than Blue and just as wide. He wasn't scared of anything or anyone not even Largo. The only thing that you had to have to control him was food and lots of it. It was the only thing he really cared about. If you didn't have enough food for him, he would probably eat you instead.

None of this was good for me or the council or the world in general.

Chapter 3

Away

After being back at home for a few days, it was a big relief. The house, the general, my little place and some peace was nice. It all felt like a bit of normality sitting in my chair in front of the fireplace. I was happy. I had forgotten how much I missed home and the simple life that I had built here for myself. But then, how much I had missed Sahara as well. I found myself sitting there talking to myself. I was still troubled by all the questions I had and I knew I had to do something about it but I wasn't ready and I didn't want to go off travelling and chase after missing wizards or even get into another fight or even war with the darkness. My fight was over or so I believed plus I wasn't really sure where I would start the jungle and the master temple was a week ride away but these issues with the code were on my mind. I just couldn't ignore them. I need to sleep on it. In the morning, I wake up early. I didn't really sleep that well. I got up and went out and over to the barn. It was chilly in the morning air and I went and found the general as usual standing there eating his hay. After a while, I got bored of talking to myself and went back in the house. *This is silly*, I thought to myself. I couldn't put this off any longer but where to start the temple was a long way off and I really didn't want to go into the capital but then maybe I didn't need to go that far. As I sat there thinking, I knew of a witch that lived closed by. May-li was another witch that I knew and another old friend. She lived in secret never using her magic power but she had always been well connected and knew everything about everything. She lived in the smaller outer part of our capital. The capital to all the kingdoms was on the edge of the sea and right in between the jungle to the east and the sand kingdom to the west. It was a massive place and it was full of everyone and anyone good bad and unfortunately the ugly. A trading post for all both in the human and magical worlds. In the morning, again I woke to the feeling of the sun and the comfort it brought to me but I knew I had to go I pack up my bag, as I planned to travel light. Then the general and I were off on an adventure.

I followed the river along past the market town through the forest for many miles till I came to the top of hill and the capital came into view. The town spread for miles across both sides of the river. It had its good and bad bits. I could see the biggest building in the middle, the royal palace, also the ship in the harbour trading their good, the pirates and the common man trying to rob anyone in sight. Lucky for me, I wouldn't need to go that far into town. May-li lived in the smallest part of the town right on the edge before you got to the mean gates which was good for me. I didn't want any questions from the king's guard or anyone knowing that I was back or what I was up to that's my business. I hadn't seen May-li for a long time, so I wasn't sure how she would take to seeing me again. I leave the general hidden just outside of town. I could trust him to stay out of sight. *Good luck to anyone who would try it on with him anyway,* I thought to myself. I made my way into town. I was wearing a big coat with a hood to cover my face and my boots were muddy so I looked like an old commoner. As Sahara had said, I wouldn't draw attention to myself, as I got closer. I could see a few people around and some horses in the stable and the inn which is exactly where I wanted to be. I walked in. No one even bothered to look at me.

Lovely, I thought to myself. I sat in the corner next to the fire warming myself up. As I sat there, I didn't feel right. I wasn't sure I was doing the right thing but before long, a young waitress girl came over.

'What you'll have?' she said.

'Beer,' I snapped. Then few moments later, she came back, put the drink down on the table and I put my coins down next to her.

'I'll give you a few more if you help me,' I asked.

'It's not that sort of a place,' she said looking at me.

'No information,' I said. She looked around to check if anyone was listening. She pulled an old rug out and stood closer.

As she wiped the table down, she bent over to get even closer to me, as I whispered to her, 'Where's May?'

To my surprise, she stood upright and rushed off. After a few minutes, a boy came walking over. He was very dirty looking no older than 12 or 15.

' Here, mister, who are ya?' he said, as I looked at him.

'Who asking?'

'Well, guv, the boss don't like ya asking questions about the mistress.'

'The mistress?' I joked. 'Well, tell him I'm an old friend. Tell him I knew her father.' With that, he was gone again and the waitress came back over. She put another beer down with a piece of paper under it.

'Drink up and get it,' she said, so I did just that. Once outside, I walked a few streets up making sure I wasn't being followed. I had to take a look at the paper. I stopped dead as it just read "the general". I turned and ran out of the town as fast as I could back to the little bit of woodland where I had left him. When I got there, I could see two horses, mine and a bright white horse with May on top. She looked at me smiled and rid of. I jumped on the general and followed her as fast as I could. We got a few miles out of town and on the bolder with the sand kingdom, as she finally slowed down and I caught up with her.

'What was all that about?' I asked, totally out of breath.

'Well, you can't be too careful these days and it's not every day that someone comes and actually knows who I really am or who knows who my father was.'

As she was still looking at me, she leant over and patted the horse. 'Hello, general,' she said.

I ignored her. 'Come on,' she said, 'we nearly home. Well it's not what I would call home but you should never judge a round doorway till you see inside.' The door was in the hillside of a dried-up old riverbed under a massive tree. It wasn't much to look at but once inside, it was nothing short of marvellous. I couldn't help but stare, as I was in a little bit of shock at how wonderful this house really was. I had forgotten all about this place. I had only been here a couple of times; the bad side to being on my own for so long. She showed me around from room to room then into one.

'Go wash,' she said, 'and I'll cook.'

Sometime later, we sat together eating and my story unfolded. I told her anything from how Largo found me in the market town to the whole council meeting at Thorberg and all about the missing wizard. May-li was a supporter of the council like me and knew only too well about the code and what it meant. She was also my friend so telling her all of this was no problem. I trusted her. After some time, she just stood up.

'I need to think,' she said and walked off back into another room. I picked up my wine and followed her. She sat in a big chair next to the fireplace. I went over and stood by the fire and warmed myself. It remembered me of home and for a second, I had forgotten everything about my silly adventure. Then she spoke again. 'So, what do you honestly think has happened to the master?' she asked me.

'I have no idea. I've not seen him in years and even then, I didn't really know him. I'm only here because Sahara and Blue asked me.'

'How is big, old Blue?' she said with a smile.

'Big and hairy,' I replied, 'and still very loud.'

She laughed. 'Oh, I miss that monkey.'

'Well, I'll tell him when I see him and since when was he ever just a monkey?' I also laughed then I looked at her. 'May, will you help me?' I asked.

'You really do need it, don't you?' she said teasing. I just stood there looking stupid.

'I honestly have no idea where to even start or what I'm really doing.'

'Then yes, I'll help you,' she said, 'get some sleep and we leave in the morning.'

Morning came. I woke early no sunshine to greet me this time which was not a good way to start the day. May-li was already up. As I got dressed and gathered my things, I walked in to the kitchen. 'Well hello there,' she said.

'Yeah morning,' I replied, 'the horses are nearly ready okay but where are we going?'

'The temple is the only place to start,' she said.

'But it's a week ride away,' I replied.

'Not by boat.'

'But that means going into the capital and you know I can't.'

'You'll be fine,' she said. I didn't like the sound of that or what she meant by it. This was definitely not going to be a good day. We left the house and rode back into town to get to the harbour. 'You have to stay on the left side of the river,' she said.

'I know that,' I snapped, 'it's not that long ago since I left this place.'

She smiled again. 'Oh really?' she cheekily replied. She was right of course. It had been over 20 years since I left the capital but I still knew every street, every turning. It all came back to me like it was yesterday. After nearly an hour, we arrived down at the docks. It was always a very busy place in the morning. All the people and ships coming and going morning noon and night but as the sun was on my face and with the smell of the sea, I felt better the docks brought back so many memories of this town. May stopped for a minute and looked around. She obviously knew what she was looking for. Then she waved. 'Come on,' she said, as we walked alone and we got closer to the ship, which wasn't the biggest I'd ever seen, it felt like someone was watching or even following us but as we were met by a rather large man mountain of a fella with a bald head and a lot tattoos. The feeling went away. He gave May-li a massive hug literally picking her up off the ground. After some minutes, he put her back down again. 'This is Baku. The ship first, mate.'

'Hello,' I said.

'Where the captain?' she asked.

'He's not here at the moment miss his…hmm…busy,' Baku said.

'Okay then, we wait.' Baku looked a bit scared but I wasn't sure if it was because of May or maybe this captain that wasn't around.

'Who is this captain then, May?' I asked.

'Captain Tai is my brother, so as you can imagine it's someone I trust. Plus, he owes me a favour. Don't worry, we will be safe with these guys.' She didn't have a brother, so I wasn't so sure. 'Come have a drink and sit in the midday sun. He'll be back shortly.'

A very loud cheer woke me up with a jump. It took me a minute to realise where I was and as the ship was just leaving the harbour. I couldn't see May and all I was really worried about was the general. Then stood in front of me was the man mountain Baku. 'Oh, you're awake. Come on then, let me show you around,' he said. As we walked, he talked a lot calling out names of the crew, that's Blackjack and Red, then these the girls Nancy and Connie and places they'd been and adventures they had. I wasn't really listening to be honest.

'Where's my horse?' I asked.

'Oh yes, the general, isn't it? What a lovely beast. Don't worry. He's nice and comfortable downstairs. This way,' he said again walking off. Down under the ship in the hold, I found him.

'Eating again, old friend.' I didn't get an answer. 'And you're ignoring me as well. What a surprise. We really in the deep end now, aren't we? And there's definitely no going back home now.' Again, I got no answer. May-li walked in.

'Maybe,' she said, 'if you call him by his real name, he might talk to you again.' The general's ears pick up. It was as if he was laughing at me. Again, I ignore her. Her horse was next to the general.

'You couldn't have picked anything a bit brighter then, I suppose.' She smiled.

'This is Star. She has been my companion for many years.'

'How did they get them on here?' I asked.

'It's my ship and it has a lot of secrets, mister?'

'Tai.'

'May said he's my friend.'

'Don't be so rude, friend,' I said, 'funny how I have never met your brother then, isn't it, May?'

'Okay so as you know, he's not my actual blood but still I'm the captain and it's my boat,' said Tai. 'And yes, she has her secrets including a door to load up horses,' he said.

'Or any other wild animals,' I said. He laughed.

'That's my business,' he replied back.

'So, tell me how much does he know about our business then, May?'

'I know nothing of your business,' he snapped at me, 'and I don't want to know. I'm a fisherman and I'm going fishing.' With that, he walked off. May looked at me and winked.

'See, we're safe here. Stop worrying.'

'Very well,' I snapped, 'but come on tell me you are too well connected to not know anything about a missing wizard and not just any wizard but the golden master of all people.'

'Look. I did hear about something that was going on in the jungle but I swear I couldn't be sure and I didn't know anything about the golden master. If I did, you know I would have gone straight to Blue myself.'

'Look,' she explained, 'you know of a dark witch called Sasha.'

'Yeah, I know her all right,' I said.

'Well, she been involved with an evil warlord known as Soren Kane head of "the black shadows",' I interrupted her.

'Yes, that's right,' she said.

'Well, they wanted to take over a part of the jungle. They wanted to start cutting down the trees and to build a new trading post for the pirates and all their ships. It would have taken away money going into the capital and given them full control and with that would have come an empire for themselves.'

'We both know the master would never allow that to happen in his part of the jungle,' she said.

'So do you think that both of them and his gang would be a match for the master and the leopard?' I replied.

'No, but you have no idea what the black shadows are like. They're very different from what you remember which is why we on our way to the temple. Now we need to see it and we need to find Nina.'

It was a good day's travel by boat but seeing May-li again was a great feeling. I had missed her. If I was honest, we had grown up together and were in trusted to the council together. It was because of her that I met Blue a very long time ago but truth was I had been on my own for so many years now that no I just didn't know the world. It had changed and I hadn't, so having May and yeah even Tai and Baku around was a nice feeling. I knew I needed all their help and more. That night, we sat around all together eating, drinking and listening to them all tell their stories. Being part of a group like that again brought back some great memories for a past that I had forgotten about. It was late before I got into bed then went to sleep.

Another morning waking up away from home was not the best feeling. Not that I had much sleep, I had forgotten what being on a boat was like and I for one couldn't wait to get off. As I went up onto the deck and with most of the others still sleeping, it was nice and peaceful up there. I felt the morning sun and the sea breeze on my face. It was a good feeling but it wasn't long after in till I heard a voice say "good morning". As I turned around, captain Tai was standing there. 'Slept well, I hope,' he said.

'No not really,' was my reply.

'Not really a sea man, are you?'

'Does it show that much?' I said. He laughed.

'So how we getting the horse out when there's no port along any part of the jungle,' I had to ask, 'and in any direction we heading?'

He laughed again. 'Oh, that's easy. As I said I'm a fisherman.' And with that, he walked off leaving me feeling even more confused than what I was before. But then, May appeared.

'Come on, let's eat,' she said. We sat and talked some more.

'So do you know if they actually build this new trading post you were talking about?'

'No, not yet,' she replied, 'but that not to say they won't.' After some time, she looked at me. 'Come on, we need to get ready.' We went back downstairs to where the horse had been. As I started to saddle the general, she just looked at me and the back door began to open. She smiled and I didn't like the look on her face one bit. She gave me my bag and then jumped up on to her horse.

'We're not,' I said.

'Yes, we are,' she said. Then with a kick, her horse bolted off and jumped straight off the back of the boat and with a massive slash, she was in the sea. Before I knew it, she was swimming to shore. I turned and looked at the captain who was laughing his head off.

'There's no way I'm doing that—' I got halfway through saying just as Baku gave the general a slap on the back. Then it was my turn and I too was off. 'Oh…my…God,' I shouted out before again with another massive slash, I too was in the sea. I could hear the cheers coming from the boat as I turned around to see capital Tai, Baku and all the crew waving and laughing. I couldn't see the funny side of it myself.

'Oh yes, how bloody funny,' I shouted back not that anyone could hear me. It only took us a couple of minutes before we managed to get up onto the beach.

'Well, that was fun,' May turned and said to me with a grin. I couldn't see it myself, as I sat there on the wet sand half drowned and with the general dripping his wet tail all over my face, I looked a right mess. But we did save ourselves five days ride and as the jungle was right there in front of us, it wasn't such a bad trip after all.

' Come on,' May shouted at me, 'we've not got time to sit around in the wet sand; we got a way to go yet.' She jumped up onto her horse and gave the boat one final wave, as she disappeared into the jungle. I tried my best to keep up.

The black shadows had already beaten us to the temple and we were going to be in for a shock. When we got there, the golden master and Mimi had tried their hardest to stop them but they were indeed no match for them. Sasha had gotten even more powerful than any of us had thought possible. Her hatred had driven her crazy and she was pure darkness now. The darkness had indeed got a plan and that it had already started meant we were behind and we didn't even know it yet. None of us knew just how far behind we would be in till it was too late. The darkness won't the sort of people to plan and that's what made Sasha so dangerous. The pieces she had to play with and the way she had Kane and all his men by her side was really worrying. I had only just started my adventure out into the world again and she was ready of all-out war.

Sasha lived completely on her own and that's how she like it. The bear the other men none of them were allowed in only Kane but even he had to be invited. She passed up and down the study bad tempered as always. The fire was burning in the corner as the old dog tried to stay out of her way. Her plans were moving on but she was just too impatient. After what felt like hours later, she heard horses approaching the castle. She ran to the window to see Kane entering the courtyard. She left the study at once and rushed down, as he walked into the hall. she snapped at him again. Take the master down to the capital and make ready but what about the snake that managed to escape, Kane said she was hurt pretty badly and she wouldn't last long out in the jungle on her own,' she said again smiling.

Sasha grinned with delight her plan indeed had worked.

'I don't care about that snake,' anyway she snapped again at him in that bad-tempered way of her. 'The master was what we were after. He's the first one out of the way which makes the council weak,' she said rubbing her hands together. 'One down and three more to go,' she said again laughing to herself. 'Now go. The forest to the north is the next target and with the master trapped in the capital, they won't know what's going on and they be down to two and we will have our advantage.'

Laughter rang throughout the castle.

Chapter 4

The Jungle

We set off and started to tackle the jungle which was very hot and hard work.

'I hope you know where we're going,' I said. 'I've never been in this part of the jungle before.'

'Yes, of course I do,' she said. 'This is the way I always come when I visit the temple.'

'Oh really? How well do you know the master then?' She gave me a look.

'I try to visit the master a couple of times a year.' Being out here with the trees, birds and animals is amazing and peaceful so different from the capital. After what felt like hours of riding through the never-ending greenery of trees, May stopped. She looked at me get off. She said, as we both jumped off our horses.

'We're nearly there,' she said, 'so keep an eye out. We have to walk in from here.' As I followed, I had to asked what we looking out for? May didn't turn around but in a low voice she just said "Mimi". *Oh great,* I thought to myself, *that bloody great big snake probably going to eat us before we've had a chance to even see the thing.* Yes, she might have been big but she can blend in with the jungle better than most of the trees. I didn't reply to her. I just kept walking, then we stopped as it came into view. We had reached a clearing and into view, came the temple. It was right in front of us. It was strangely quiet.

'No monkeys,' May said.

'No birds,' I replied. May drew her sword, as I had my bow. We left the horse on the edge of the trees and walked towards the temple.

'Where's that snake?' she said, as we entered the temple where it was really quiet. Nothing seemed out of place but there was no sign of Mimi, the snake or Nina, the leopard, either or in fact anything living. We searched the whole temple for a good hour and found absolutely nothing.

'I'll get the horses,' I said, 'we better stay here tonight.' May looked as confused as I did but agreed there was food in the temple fruit, bread even wine. We found a place up high and hind. The horses out of the way, as we sat and talked by a fire I had made. Something was clearly troubling May. I told her that there were just too many questions. First, the master was missing then the leopard now that great big snake.

'Mimi,' she said, 'she has a name.'

'Yeah, I know,' I said, as I walked over and put my hand on her arms. 'She does, the same as Nina and the master, though I don't actually know it,' I said, as May laughed. 'So, something has happened here and there wasn't really any clues but for the temple to be this empty, it must have been bad but what? And with who? And why?'

'Questions, questions, hang on,' May said.

'Yeah, they're a lot of questions but maybe there's an answer in there. What did Sahara say to you at this meeting?'

'Well, she said they didn't know where he was and that no one had seen him and when I asked about Nina they didn't really answer as they didn't know that either.'

'So, the master is missing but Nina might not be,' May said.

'What?' I replied. 'That leopard goes everywhere with him his own bodyguard everyone knows that. How can he be missing and not her?'

'Look, when the master is safe and at the temple, Nina goes off on her own. She lives and breathes in the jungle so maybe the master left without her this once which is why he's missing.'

'Okay so where is she then?' I asked.

'At first light, I'll take you to her real home. I'm so glad I was the first person you came to for help,' she said to me, as the fire was dying down and it was getting late.

'So am I,' I said back to her, 'unfortunately, there's not many of us old guards left in this world now, May, and I'm glad you didn't turn me to stone if I'm honest.'

'I wouldn't.' She laughed.

'Mmmm. I honestly wasn't sure the last time we were together with Sahara and—'

'No, you have to let it go now,' she interrupted. 'It wasn't your fault then and it's not now, you know that. I know that, and she definitely knows it, you saved us all.'

'Not all,' it was my turn to interrupt her.

'You did what you could and nothing then and now could ever change that. Go to sleep,' she said in her calming voice and with her smile, 'I am and I always will be your friend and a follower to you, my general.'

The next morning, we were up and out early. You don't really have a choice in the jungle. It was back to being noisy with the birds flying around. The temple itself was still too quiet for our liking. It was like none of the animals wanted to come near it, as it all felt a bit strange and out of character for the whole place as if the creatures all know the master had gone. We got the horses ready and headed off. Unfortunately, there was more walking to start with. It was hot and slow going. I followed May through the jungle. It was as if she could see the pathway there in front of her without there actually being a path. I knew she wasn't telling me something about this place. I had known her far too long and been in far too many situations like this not to know her but I happily followed her. I trusted her with my life and had done too many times. It wasn't long before we could hear something and she even asked me, 'Do you hear that water?'

I said, 'Yeah, it's the river.'

'There's no river in the jungle everyone knows that.' She laughed again. 'Oh, dear God, you really hadn't been here before, have you?' she said. I ignored her because I hated it when she was always right. We literally stopped and in front of us indeed was a river. It was fast flowing and very wide.

'Please don't tell me we jumping into more water on horseback.'

She laughed again. 'Oh no, not this time.'

'Good,' I said, and stop laughing at me.'

'Come on, we can ride from here,' she said, as she jumped up on her bright white horse. More good news. I was liking this. As we followed the river edge around for a good mile or so, then May shouts out "there" as she points over. I could see a waterfall. We carry on riding till we get really close and she stopped there. A cave at the base of it behind the water.

'Wait here,' she said. 'I'm going to have a look.' Before I could stop her, she was off and I nervously waited with the horses. After a few minutes, she comes back out. 'I've found her.'

'Who?' I ask. 'Nina?'

'Come on,' May said, as she led her horse inside. I jumped off the general and followed her. Inside was dark to start. Then it opened up into a massive cave with holes in the top. That lit the place up by the sunlight. Then right in the back, I got to see her and for only the 2rd or 3rd time in my life, Sass Mimi Siss at me.

'Sssso it'ssss you who they've have pick to find my missteer.'

'Hello, Mimi. It's good to see you are safe.'

'Yessss jusssst I wassss lucky.'

'Stop talking. You need to rest now.' May-li was on her knees and attended to Mimi's wounds.

'Who did this to you?' I asked.

'Not now,' May-li snapped at me not in a good way.

'But we need to know, May. I'm a friend to the witch and a supporter to the council. We both are.'

'I know who you both are,' she said.

'We need to know what happened and where the master is.'

'NOT NOW,' again May-li snapped at me. Then we heard it. A very loud BOOM from outside. SSSSSSSS. Nina rose up. I'd never seen her that tall before.

'Get behind me,' she said.

47

'No,' May said, drawing her sword again. I grabbed my bow, drew it back, as we could just make out a shadow in the entrance than laughter. Sss sss sss from the snake, as she lowered her self-down almost to a bow. Me and May still weren't sure who it was. Then that hairy face appeared and that booming voice.

'Hello, May,' Blue said, as he walked in. She dropped her sword and ran over to give him the biggest hug. 'Mimi,' he said, 'very nice to see you.'

'Well, thanksssss,' she said.

I breathed in relief. 'It's good to see you again, Blue.' As I walked over to him.

'Yes, old friend. We're here to help you,' he said, as another two gorillas walked in behind him. *Wow*, I thought to myself again. It had been too long since I had seen them all. We sat down and I explained how we won't be getting anywhere. We still have more questions than answers and still had no clues about the master or Nina. The temple had been completed empty and we only found Mimi because May-li knew about this cave. May walked over.

'How's Mimi doing?' Blue asked.

'She's resting now. She'd been in a battle with someone or something but she didn't say anything about who.'

'What sort of battle?' Blue asked.

'To me, it looks like she was attacked by something big.'

'Big?' I asked. 'How big?' May paused for a second and we both looked at her.

'May, what is it?' Blue asked.

'There's only one creature I know that could have done that to her.'

'Who, May, who?' I said.

Again, she looked at both of us and I couldn't believe my ears when I heard her say his name: Whistleroot. Blue looked even more surprised than I did and I nearly fell off the rock. I was sitting and my heart was pounding in my chest. The fear from that day all felt like it was yesterday. Blue rose up.

'Okay, look you two, let me worry about that bear if indeed he is back. I have news now about the black shadows. They have been seen in a small town on the edge of the jungle looting and just causing the usual trouble but she was also with them.'

'Sasha?' I said. 'So, it's true the witch and the warlord are working together but that doesn't explain anything.'

'Maybe,' Blue said, 'but this isn't good. When definitely parts of the darkness work together like this, it doesn't normally end well and people get hurt,' Blue said. 'We'll stay here, take care of Mimi and get her back to the temple. You guys need to go find the witch,' Blue said again.

'And you're going to need some more help from who?'

'I asked from a friend who has also been searching though this jungle for Nina,' Blue explained. 'He's a black panther called Kai. It was Kai that first came to me about the master and Nina being missing. He's been searching ever since, and it's only because of him that I knew where this cave was. You only just beat me here,' he said.

'Okay so where can we find this panther?' I asked again.

'Carry on following the river north. He will find you,' Blue said. 'May-li, show him how you know the master and he will trust you. No questions.' So we left the waterfall behind and our adventure continued.

As we rode through the jungle, I just couldn't help but think of Sahara. Seeing her again had made me realise just

49

how long I'll been on my own. I had run away from something that wasn't my fault but the guilt I felt for what had happened was real and running away from that hadn't helped.

'Oi you awake?' May-li shouted at me.

'What, me? Yes of course, I'm awake,' I replied.

'Well, come on then. You're lagging behind. We still got a way to go yet, okay?'

'Okay,' I said. As we rode up hill and away from the river, the jungle thinned out. The view was incredible. The sounds and smells of the jungle were truly amazing and for a second, I'd forgotten all about our adventures.

'Do you know where we going?' I asked.

'Yes of course, I do,' May answered. 'Well, I think I do,' she added in a low voice. We went on a bit further on and came up to the biggest tree I had ever seen.

In the tree, asleep was a panther. We stopped and May shouted out, 'Hello there.'

He opened his eyes. 'Well, hello. Someone brought me lunch,' he said with a grin.

'Try it,' I said, drawing my bow back. He laughed.

'Stop it,' May snapped at me.

'Are you Kai, the black panther, that I was told could help us?'

'No, I'm not him,' he said. 'My name is Char.'

And as he got ready to jump out of the tree, 'I am,' said another voice from behind us. As we turned around, another panther stood there.

'This one was much bigger, Kai,' Char said.

'I see them first; they're my prey.' Kai just stood and looked on. He didn't move an inch.

'Yes, they are,' Kai said, 'but before you eat them, may I ask you, young lady, who are you?'

'I'm no one special,' May-li said.

'Oh really? Well, if that really is true, you are going to be his lunch.' Char laughed and jumped out the tree straight at May-li. She just managed to jump out of the way but he had her corner. Not me or even her horse Star could help her now.

'Use the ring,' Kai shouted at her. She looked up at him and froze for a second. I've never seen her so scared before. May-li put her hand in her pocket and pulled out a ring. She put it on and closed her eyes. Char saw this as his opportunity and with that grin, he jumped right at her. She opened her eyes and blasted him with her magic sending him flying through the air straight back into the side of the tree that he came out of. I was just as shocked as the panther. In all the years I had known her, I had never seen her do that. Char looked at us and ran off. Kai still standing there laughed. 'Well done, witch. Nice to see you.' May-li smiled back.

'That felt good,' she said.

'And so it should,' Kai said, 'you are a witch, are you not?'

'Yes but—' she tried to say.

'But nothing,' Kai interrupted her. 'Blue has told me all about you two. Who you are and what you both are. I've been following you since you left the temple. I spotted Blue and spoke with him while you were both in Nina's cave. I hear Mimi is better now thanks to you. Anyone who treats the animals of this world like you do is a friend of mine,' he said.

The black shadows were indeed in a little town. On the edge of the jungle to the north, they had moved in and were course trouble. There were around 20 men plus a pack of six wolves and a couple of lions. They had ridded and smashed the place up. They had drunk the wine and had eaten all the food. They had also rounded up all the town's people. Kane or the bear were nowhere to be seen but the witch was there all right. After her first plan had worked at the temple, she was on to the next bit and we were still playing catch up not that we had any clue of that, the trading post in the jungle was nothing compared to Sasha's real plan. She wanted to take over and not just the capital or the council but the whole world as we knew it. Blue's home in the north was her next target where Blue was there or not didn't matter just knowing she could get to his family would be enough to draw him out. Blue was in big trouble and none of us even knew it.

'Come on, we have a wizard to find,' he said. As he walked off, I just looked at May in total shock.

'What has just happened?' I asked her. I didn't get an answer. We started off on our way again. I couldn't help but feel home was even further away than ever now. Fortunately for me, the jungle was hot and the sun gave me comfort as I could feel it on my back. We rode of a few hours in the afternoon heat. We came back down and into where the river flowed. We stopped to let the horses drink. Kai told us that we need to find a place to rest before it got too late, so we rode a bit more up river till we found a nice little spot. Kai had a look around, May attended to the horses and I got on with the fire. May took the first watch as Kai slept in the tree. I had no problem falling asleep as I didn't sleep well on the boat but it wasn't long before I was being woken up again.

'Your turn,' May said. I got up, put some more wood on the fire, as May went to sleep. As I sat there, the feeling of guilt came back and the bad memories of Sahara. What had happened between us was just something that I couldn't shake.

May might have said it wasn't my fault. Sahara herself didn't want to talk about it at the council meeting but it troubled me and if I was honest, it always had. By trying to save her, I nearly killed her. They called me a hero at the time but I didn't feel that way to the point where it drove me away from everyone and anything that I ever loved. I laid there thinking or more like daydreaming as Kai jumped down from the tree and scared me to death.

'Oh, so you are awake then,' he said. 'I thought you of all people should know that sleeping at their post at night is never a good sign.'

'I wasn't asleep,' I replied.

'No, but you weren't watching out either,' he snapped back at me. 'I expect better from you of all people.'

'I'm not that person anymore.' I jumped up and walked off. I just didn't want to hear it from all these people. Blue, Sahara, May now this panther all thinking they know me, what I am or who I am. I was really getting sick of it after a few minutes of standing in the cold, dark night of the jungle. I got over it and went back to the others. May was still sleeping get some rest.

Kai said, 'I'll keep watch from now on.' As morning broke, the jungle once again came alive with the sounds of the birds and the animals. It was all around us with the morning sunshine. We all got ready and moved on but again, I lagged behind. My mind was full of all the rubbish from the night before and from what was now a week since the meeting from me leaving my home, we didn't have any answers to the many questions we had. Yes, we had made a few new friends on the way, which was always a good thing and yes, we knew what we were looking for now and yeah, I knew that I had no choice but to carry on going. Kai disappeared out of sight for a while as we keep going through the jungle. He moved through the trees with such ease that we didn't really know where he was half the time. Me and May just kept going. Then out of nowhere, he appeared again.

'Come on,' he said, 'it's not much further now.' Then he was gone again. May asked if I was okay. I wasn't really sure if I was honest and I think she knew it being out here was something she was used to but for me, it wasn't. I felt lost and unsure for myself. But like normal, I didn't get much of a choice. Then again out of the jungle, Kai appeared.

'Hurry this way,' he said. So we followed him as we changed direction. Something wasn't right.

'What is it?' I said. No reply.

'Come on,' he shouted, as he disappeared again. Then we came up to a clearing in the trees and we could see we had reached the edge of the jungle. On the west side, the jungle gave away to grasslands and in the distance, there was the small town that Blue had mentioned which looked very much like it was burning.

Chapter 5

The Witches Dual and Beyond

We left the horses and went down for a closer look. We could see the black shadows had clearly taken over. The thick smoke was in the air from some of the building being on fire. There were people in cages and wolves running around who were fighting over old bones? We couldn't see Sasha or Kane but then there wasn't any sign of the master or Nina either. Kai got a little bit closer smelling the air for any signs of Nina's scent. After a few minutes, he crept back over to us. He didn't look at all happy.

'Well?' I asked.

'I couldn't be sure if either of them are actually in there,' he said.

'So now what do we do if we go in and it's all been for nothing?'

'We could rise the alarm.'

'Then Sasha will know we are on to her and I don't want to die for absolute no reason.' May just sat there and didn't say a word. I could tell she was thinking about something.

'May?' I said. 'What's the plan, old friend?' She just looked at me.

'I'm supposed to say that to you,' she replied.

'Yeah well, I'm not that person anymore so.'

'You keep saying,' snapped the panther, 'but sooner or later, you will need to be. You can't ignore this forever. You can't just ignore the past or indeed forget who you truly are.'

May looked at me. 'You've not even unwrapped your sword.'

'I don't need that,' I half-heartedly replied.

'Well, then why bring it? Why find me? Or even come all this way to fine someone you don't even know in the first place.' Her face, the angry she felt was clear to see. I couldn't run away any more. It was time to face the truth.

'Look,' Kai said, 'we go in at night. Let's go,' and with that, we went back to the cover of the edge of the jungle. Once there, Kai said we going to need some more help and again, he was gone. May unpacked her horse, the ring, her sword, everything she needed to get into a real fight and she looked ready of it as well. I wasn't but it was my turn. I walked over to the general, patted him down. I take out my bow. All the arrows I had and yes for the first time in an absolute age, my sword.

'Hello, old friend,' I found myself saying again. It had been a week for meeting old friends. I felt hot and totally unready standing with all my gear on. I had become fat and unfit for battle but I didn't really get a choice and deep down in my heart, I could feel the excitement of it all. The rush that I had been ignored for so long.

Out of the evening sky, Kai appeared once again out of breath. He didn't say nothing. He just laid there looking out towards the town. Me and May were all ready and sat down next to him. I didn't really know what to expect. After a few seconds, he spoke, 'Follow me.' We slowly crept back down towards the town. Then he stopped. 'Wait for it,' he said. I still had no idea what was going on but we heard it well before we could see it. Thunder or what sounded like it coming from the jungle. Then they came into sight a herd of 50 elephants stampeding down the hill. The shadows couldn't hear it. At first, they were all having too much fun in the town. 'They're going to clear us a whole and hopefully chase a few of them off,' Kai said, 'then we going in.' It didn't take long. The elephants really could move when they wanted to. Before we knew it, they were crashing through the town. The noise and commotion it caused was like nothing I'd seen before. Then Kai jumped up. 'Now,' he shouted and we followed on after him. The fight was on. May drew her sword and attacked anyone that was brave enough to run at her. I shot my bow with my best aim. The elephants did a great job of clearing the place out as they went through but with all the noise and smoke, it was hard to see everything. Then Kai was fighting with a dozen wolves and I dealt with the last of the shadows.

Just as I noticed, May going into the biggest building in the town but then she didn't come out and I couldn't help her for a minute. I was busy. There were more men than I had first thought. The time had come. As I drew my sword, the battle really did start all over again for me. I managed to fight off a few more of them to start with but it wasn't easy. I could feel the fight in me coming back. Then two more as I edged closer to where May was. She still hadn't come back out and with all the commotion, it was hard to see but I didn't have time. With another two more, there really were a lot more shadows than I thought. Kai was still busy with the wolves but by then, I had just managed to reach the building where May had gone into. I entered. I went down some steps to find May on her knees.

It was like being back in that cave again as she was attending a very hurt looking leopard. She hadn't notice behind her was a lion in the background ready to attack her. I run over still holding my sword out and after a very bloody fight with the lion hurting myself badly in the process, I had finally buried the guilt I had been carrying around with me. Kai walked in.

'Well done,' he said to me, 'you have finally waken up I see. Good because we are going to need the other half of you. We are not out of this yet.' He turned and walked over to Nina. He licked her. 'Hello, my love,' he said softly. She looked up and grinned at him. 'How is she?' he asked May.

'Weak,' she said.

'Can you walk, my love?' Kai said.

'Yes,' Nina replied in a low voice. We all helped her up. I went back up the steps first followed by the panther and the leopard May last. As we got there, Nina collapsed to the ground but what was waiting for us was much worse. Sasha was standing there dressed all in black as she normally was. There were a couple of the wolves left. I wasn't sure if this was good or bad. Kai turned to May.

'This is your time now, my girl,' he said. She walked out in front, as Sasha stepped out to. The witches' dual was on.

'I'm May-li, witch to the light,' she said.

'I'm Sasha, witch to the darkness,' she said.

Then together, they both said, 'I'm bound by a code and will not kill.'

Wow, I thought I had seen magical duals before but never so close and with someone I was so close to. May had been my friend for so long. I looked at Kai. His focus was all on May. She had her ring on and Sasha had her wand in her hand. The fight started with flashes of lightning and bangs of fire.

Sasha had that angry look on her face. May looked a bit calmer. Then more flashes. Before long, Sasha changed into a tiger and charged straight at May. She instantly responded changing herself into a bird and flying up high into the air. Sasha did the same then more flashes and bangs. The noise and the lighting looked amazing. High above us. Kai saw this as our opportunity to escape. He looked at me and shouted, 'Now,' charging at the wolves. I followed, once again drawing my sword but it didn't take much. The wolves weren't interested in getting in to enough fight and ran off. After that, it was my turn to help Nina up as we made a run for it back up to the edge of the jungle. Once we were out of town and back up the hill, the sky was still alight with the bangs and flashes of fire. The witches were really going at it. Once we got there, Nina rested and I got on the general.

'Where you going?' Kai asked.

'I'm going back to town,' I said. 'I need to find May.'

'She will be fine,' he said, 'she needs to do this on her own.' Kai walked over and whispered something to Star, as he let her go. We need to move. The shadows will regroup and be looking for us now. May had landed back in the town and Sasha wasn't far behind and the fighting continued. The two witches had now changed into bears and were wrestling with each other on the ground of the town. Not that there was much of the town left. The pair threw punches and pushed each other around. Sasha put May through a wooden door. Before May knocked Sasha into an old wooden cart that was on fire. After a few more minutes, they changed back into themselves both out of breath, sweating and both wounded. It was clear there wasn't going to be a winning here. Sasha took her leave jumping on a wolf and riding off into the dark of the night.

May fell to the ground. Just as Star appeared, May got herself on her horse and did the same.

After hours of walking back through the jungle, I, Kai and Nina arrived back at the temple. Blue, the other gorillas and a better-looking Mimi were there waiting for us. I almost fell off my horse from the night activates, as I was hurt with blood running down my arm. Plus, I was hot and very tired from the last few days and the battle we had just been in. My mind was full of worry, as I just couldn't stop thinking about May and if she was all right.

'Rest up, old friend,' Blue said, as he helped me get off the horse. I sat down and soon fell asleep.

'Kai,' Blue said, 'tell me everything.' Kai, who was helping Nina get comfortable, turned around and walked over to where Blue was and the pair sat together talking.

'Well,' he said, 'May used the ring and got herself into a witches' dual with Sasha.'

'Wow,' Blue said. 'You don't hang around,' he said with a smile.

'No, we don't have time for that, old friend, and from what I saw, she handled it very well.'

'What about him?' Blue said again.

'Well, he hasn't forgotten how to use that sword of his even if age and being on his own has made him fat and slow.'

'Thank God,' Blue said.

'And it appears he learnt how to use a bow while he's been away.'

'That's good,' Blue said again with a grin, 'we going to need them both fighting fit if this gets as bad as Largo said.'

'Yeah, I agree,' Kai replied.

'Now you better rest up too, Kai. You are all safe here now,' Blue said once more. Before long, all but Blue and the other gorillas were asleep. May-li's horse, Star, had been walking back through the jungle. May was on top half-asleep and hurt, as Star carefully found her way all the back to the temple. As they arrived back, Blue lifted a hurt and bleeding looking May off the horse and gently put her down. It was the animals' turn to attend to her as Blue did the best he could. SSSSSSSS the snake rose up again.

'Ssssomeone coming,' she said. Blue sent the other two gorillas up to the top of the temple to have a look but outside was the white carriage and the dogs of the silver witch. Blue breathed a sigh of relief, as he went outside to greet them hello.

'Blue,' Sahara said with a hug.

'Hello, my lady,' he replied, 'they have found Nina and someone else.'

'Who?' she asked.

'Someone who's been missing a long time.' They both walked in together.

'My lady,' Kai said, 'very pleased to see you again.'

'Kai, I'm glad you and Nina are back together again,' she said with that soft voice before turning around and looking she spotted it. She just stood and looked at me. I was half-asleep.

'Is that—'

'Yes,' interrupted Blue.

'My God, how did you ever get him to hold that sword again?'

Kai smiled. 'I didn't.' As she walked over, she could see that I was bleeding.

'He's hurt,' she said. As she bent down next to me, it woke me up with a shock.

'Am I dreaming or am I dead?' I said half asleep.

'Neither,' she said very bluntly. 'Now hold still.' She undid my belts to take off my sword and where I had my arrows, pulled my shirt up. 'Lion,' she said. I just nodded. 'It's not too deep. A good wash would help clean that out. Come on. I'll help you up, please.'

Blue said, 'Let me, my lady.'

'Take him down to the river and throw him in.' I could hear Kai laughing, as I was helped away.

'Now,' she said turning to Kai, 'tell me all about this witch dual,' she asked. First, he told her all about Char and the ring then the fight with Sasha word for word every detail.

'That's great,' she said, 'finally she's been a captain in the guard of too many years. She is a witch and we need her to be exactly that.' Sahara's guard got May into her carriage and they had both left. By the time I managed to get out of the river and back to the temple, Blue told me that Sahara's plan was to take her to her home, look after her and train her in the ways of the witches. I didn't like it but who was I to argue with a council member.

'So now what? Blue, I still have no idea about the master who I'm supposed to be finding. That what you all wanted, wasn't it? Not too fine a leopard but I've done that not to get into a bloody fight oh but I've also done that I'm tired, hurt and still nowhere nearer to going home.'

'Yes, I know all of that, old friend, but you must realise that might have happened at some point.' He of course was right. I knew full well if I left my home and started this, it wasn't going to be just a few days or a 'oh there he is' sort of trip. I'm in deep now and there was no going back. I walked off and went back up to where me and May had stayed in the temple a few nights ago, fell asleep and didn't wake up until morning.

The next morning, when I did wake up, I felt a lot better. I went outside. That sun was warm and the birds were their usual noisy selves. Kai wasn't there but Blue was. Nina was still sleeping and Mimi looked well.

'So, big guy,' I said, 'what is the plan?' Largo believes that the darkness has planned something big. The master was only the beginning. Sasha and the shadows have been getting bigger every day. More and more gangs are joining them. It's like she growing an army. Men, animals even a few other witches,' he said, 'they have all been seen with her.'

'So, is she in control, and what of this Soren Kane?' I said.

'Oh, he's there all right. Just because we've not seen him, don't let that fool you.'

'Okay so if the dark forces are moving, what are the council doing about it?'

'That's where you come in.'

Oh god, I thought to myself. 'Why does this not sound good,' I said, as I rubbed my head. 'What do you need me to do now?'

'I'm sorry, old friend. Me and even Sahara would never ask you this if we didn't honestly believe we needed it.'

'What, Blue?' I regrettably asked.

'We need you to go to the queen.' As soon as he said the words, my heart almost stopped.

'Oh great,' I said out loud, 'this just keeps getting better and better. You know she shot me on sight, right? You do know that I won't even get in the doorway. I just managed to go through the capital without being seen once. I won't get away with that again, Blue.'

'Come on, look,' he snapped. 'I realise this is hard and not ideal but yes—'

'Okay, okay,' I interrupted once more, 'you're only asking because you have to.'

'Rest up another day,' Blue said, 'then pack up and tomorrow Kai will take you to the capital's eastern gate.' Again, I didn't really have the choice. I walked out of the temple and a little into the jungle. I felt calm thoughts of home, and May even Sahara. Yeah, I had been on my own but I did have to admit I missed the adventure. The general had followed me a little way. Almost knocked me over as he came up behind me.

'Oi,' I said, 'what you doing?' But again nothing. 'Still not talking to me, are you?' No reply. As I got closer to the river, I found an old tree. I sat down in the midday sun and enjoyed the peace. A few minutes later, I was asleep once more.

But my mind wouldn't rest. I couldn't help but relive the past. The very day that I had been running away from. It was 20 years ago to be exact. The king of the capital and indeed of all the kingdoms was called the emerald king. He was my king. He was a very old but wise man. Kind, caring and a loyal king. He had the full support of both the council and of his people. He knew them all very well even Sahara's mother back when she was on the council. He was a proud father himself of two children, the eldest a daughter and a son. Now there were many parts to our world from the jungle to the east and the sand kingdom to the west. The mountains coving the north and flat grasslands and forests spread throughout the middle. There were many lords and leader to all their parts but the king was the king. He had full control of it all and he worked hard to make sure that the world stayed a safe and good place to live and it was for the most part. The king knew all about the darkness all right. He like Largo had been fighting it for many years with great cost to him. He lost his father in battle and he himself had been in many wars all over our earth. The king himself had grown weak with every fight and of course age, in the end, he could barely walk let alone ride his horse anymore which meant he couldn't travel around like he used to. That bothered him greatly. Now as I may have mentioned, something happened to me that made me go live a boring life on my own. It's about time I explained that particular tale. There was once an evil wizard call Barus at that time. The darkness didn't really have any control. The king had kept it in check but Barus had grown so jealous of the king that he had a plan to draw the king out and away from the capital. Barus along with his gang ambushed and attacked the home of one of the king's dear friends, a witch call Indiana. She was a beautiful woman and a very powerful witch. She at the time was a member of the council and Sahara's mother. She tried her hardest to fight off the gang and was locked in a magic dual with the wizard for a full day in till Largo flew in to help, rescue her or so he thought. It was Largo they wanted all along. The battle with Indiana was only a decoy. As soon as the dragon had landed, the trap was sprung and Largo was caught up with ropes and nets and he couldn't escape.

The emerald king heard about this and sent his own royal guard which included his general who of course was me and the captain May-li to help. We rode hard for a full day and then went straight into the battle. Forty of us went in and the fighting lasted well into the night. I found Indiana hiding. She was hurt and on her own or so I thought. She wouldn't leave her home as if she was protecting something. It was then that I first met Sahara. She was the prettiest woman I had even seen. But I had my orders and I told Indiana that I had to get her out of there.

' My lady,' I said to her, 'you are more important than any of us and it's my king's wish that I get you safely back to the capital.' As we made our way out of her home, May and a couple of our men were close by. I told her to take Indiana and Sahara and get them both back to the king and that I would go and help Largo but Indiana wouldn't go. She was the only one who could help Largo so she made me promise that I would protect her daughter. 'Yes, of course,' I replied, when she asked me, 'whatever it takes.'

'No,' she said grabbing me by my arm and holding me tight, 'promise me?' I can still remember the look in her eyes as she asked.

I looked at her and with all my heart, I said, 'I general Marko Vas-ta leader to the emerald king royal guard promise to protect your daughter, Sahara, with all my life.' The pain I feel when I hear myself saying those words in my head is what drives me away. I told her as I looked into my eyes.

'Thank you,' she said. Then she hugged her daughter and left us. Indiana died that day by saving Largo but there's more to it than that and the story doesn't end there. As we made our way out of there and tried to escape, we were cornered by Whistleroot, a very big and nasty looking black bear. He had served the darkness for a long time and everyone knew who he was. Standing seven-foot-tall and with his metal armour on and so the fighting carried on. I tried my hardest to get us all out of there but the bear killed six of my men and Sahara now carried the scars from the very bear. I did everything I could to get her back to the capital and was made a hero. Barus was never seen of again but after that, the guilt and the fear I felt for what had happened to both Sahara and her mother drove me mad and I've carried it around with me for all these years. I gave up on my post. I had given up on my king and on myself. I left and went off to be on my own. Sahara never blamed me and she told me many times after that, but I left. Unfortunately, I didn't listen. I just couldn't bare the shame that I felt. I had failed her. I had failed on the promise that I had made to her mother Indiana. A few years later, I heard that the king had died which hurt me deeply. I couldn't help but feel that I had abandoned my post and my king for selfish reason. The king's eldest daughter was made queen and as she never liked me, she had blamed me for his death, which of course I didn't have anything to do with. She always claimed he died a broken man all because of me.

I woke up with a jump and was sweating. It had only been a dream but then maybe not as it was real. It had all been so very real all those years ago but for me in my mind, it was like it was yesterday.

Unfortunately, like most things in the jungle, the peace didn't last that long. Monkeys high up in the trees were passing by one of which landed right on top of my head with a thud.

'Oh, so sorry, my lord.'

'Lord?' I said. Now it was my turn to laugh. 'I'm not really a lord.'

'Oh well then maybe a knight then.' This little monkey went on and on walking around and waving his arms about.

'Look, little fella, I'm just trying to enjoy the peace and the sun.'

'Oh yes, yes, yes,' he replied.

'But you know what?'

'Oh, what now?'

'This is the jungle. It's never quiet in the jungle,' he said with a massive grin.

'You telling me.'

He stuck out his little hand. 'The name's Marley.'

'Well, hello,' I said back, shaking his hand…Still shaking.

'Well, you are,' he said, 'back.'

'Oh well, I'm.'

'Yes!' he said again.

'My name is Marko.'

'Very pleased indeed,' he said again, still shaking my hand.

The general looked at me shaking his head with that oh not enough unwanted pet look. I finally got Marley to let go.

'So, what brings you to the jungle?'

'That's my business not yours,' I snapped.

'Okay, okay. You humans are so uptight all the time. No fun nope, nope, nope.' He was still waving his arms around, as he spoke. Then just as quickly as he came, he had gone.

I went back to the temple. Kai and Nina had gone off and Mimi was cured up inside the temple where it was cooler for her and out of the midday heat. I got all my things ready to travel again and as I sat there eating, I couldn't help but think of my little house and how far I had come. But I'm not sure I was going to like the next bit seeing the queen and being on my own just didn't feel right though I did like the fact that it was warm here in the south of the jungle and not winter like it would be at home.

Chapter 6

The Capital

The next morning again, I woke up in the temple. I walked out into the morning sunshine. I was just getting used to it here with all the sounds and smells but it was time to leave. I didn't get much sleep at first. I just laid there for what felt like hours I couldn't get the thought out of my mind how the queen really wasn't going to have a good day when she sees me back in the capital and I wasn't really too sure why Blue even wanted me to go back there. The new queen would have let any of the council members in with no problem so why send me? Morning came.

That big, old voice. 'Yes, it is Blue.' I replied. 'So, what do you need me to do?' I asked.

'I need you to go to jail! Once you in the town, put the horse in the stables. Don't carry any weapons with you. Get yourself into trouble and let them catch you. Once you're in the jail, you can lay low. It's been 20 years so many of the guards won't even know you anymore.'

'Oh great,' I said. 'I'm the most infamous general that the kingdom's ever had.'

'Brilliant, that's not important, Marko,' Blue said. Hearing him say my name for the first time made me stop...I had not heard him say that in a long time.

'Okay once I'm in jail, then what?'

'I can't be sure but you'll know it when you see it.'

Very helpful, I thought to myself. I got ready. Then me and the general were off again on the next part of our adventures. The path through the jungle in the morning sun was hot and hard going. Not like back in the forest near home. Oh, my home, my chair. I could feel it all now. Kai again travelled through the tree with a lot more ease than my poor horse. After a couple of hours, the pathway became a lot bigger. Kai sat waiting for me to catch up right.

He said to me, 'This is where I leave you. Follow it west for a mile and you will see the capital and the gateway.'

'Thanks,' I said.

'No problem,' he replied.

'No, I mean it. Thank you.' He just grinned and jumped back into the tree and out of sight.

Not one for goodbyes then, I thought. I rode off along the pathway. It wasn't long before the capital came into view. The smell hit me first. Dirty air, nothing like the jungle. As I approached the gateway, I felt a thud on my head again. It was Marley.

'What the bloody hell you doing?'

'Hey, hey, hey,' he said in his funny voice. 'I've never been to the capital before.'

'So, you not coming in now either?' I said but it was too late. I grabbed him and stuck him in my bag before the guards noticed. I put my hood up and entered into town. I walked along and found the stable. Once inside, I put my horse away and then took off my coat, wrapped my sword back up and as I grabbed my bag, the monkey popped out waving his arms around again.

'Why do that?' he said. 'I almost died. Do you know how dark it is in there.'

'Marley, it's a bag. It was either that or the dinner table.'

'Now please what do you want?'

'I'm busy.'

'Oh yes, busy with stuff that is not my business,' he replied.

I just look at him. 'Okay, okay I'll stand guard of the horse,' he said again with a grin. Very important job for Marley. I grabbed my bag and left him to it. There was something strange about that monkey but in a good way. I couldn't help but think Blue was responsible for him following me. As I left the stables, I wandered through the streets. I couldn't help but feel a bit lost. Blue didn't really explain. He only said get into trouble and go to jail but I wasn't too sure how to do that. I had been the general to the royal guard not a street guard or even a thief. The market was probably a good place to start. It was big and on the riverfront, as I made me way over there, the thought of May popped in to my head. I knew she would be okay with Sahara but I always worried. She had been my captain and my friend for so long. I had only just found her and now she was gone again.

The market was its usual busy self but it was bigger then. I had remembered as I walked through. I wasn't really looking and I still didn't really know how I was going to get myself into the jail. Then a hand grabbed my arm.

'Marko,' a voice said, as I turned to see a little, old lady standing there.

'Mrs French?' I said, as she hugged me.

'It's been a long time. Does she know you're back in town?'

'No,' I replied.

'Come on inside then. We need to talk.' Mrs French along with her husband had sold fish in the market for as long as I could remember. It was the best seafood in all the capital. Everyone knew her. She had been around that long. She knew all about the council the good and the bad and all about the kingdoms. We sat and she made tea.

'You're looking well, Marko, but it's been a long time since I've seen you down here in the market.'

'Yes, Mrs French, it has indeed been a very long time. How is Mr French?' She stopped and didn't say nothing for a second. 'Oh,' I said, 'I'm sorry about that.'

'So, what you really doing here?'

'Blue asked me to come back.'

'Oh,' she said, 'I need to get into the jail.'

'Why in heavens would you do that?'

She said no idea. I replied, 'If I'm honest…'

She laughed. 'You still jumping into the deep end, aren't ya, Marko?'

'Yeah, suppose I am.'

'Well then, let's get you in jail,' she said with a grin. I didn't know what she meant but I soon found out now.

'Marko, you could go rob someone in the market or get into a fight. But why go to all that bother when you can just go in the back door.' As she said that, a young girl walked in. 'Oh Olivia, just the very person. This is Marko, a very old friend of mine. He needs to go to jail. Could you be a darling and show him the back door.'

'Yes of course, Mrs French,' she said.

'Good girl. Marko, you can trust her. Now go on your way. I do hope you be okay.' I stood up and thanked her with a hug. I left with my newest travelling companion; a girl called Olivia. We were making our way back through the market. Once more, she wasn't the lovely young girl that I had thought.

'Look,' she said, 'call me Liv. Follow me. Do as ya told and I'll get ya to jail.' I was a bit shocked but as we moved through the capital down alleyways and up over roofs. It was clear she knew the town in a completely different way to me. Within minutes, we were at the jail. Something that would have taken me an hour. Liv showed me to a tunnel that led down under the town jail. 'Carry on to the end, do a right and then you'll come up right in the middle of the jail,' she said.

'Oh okay. Well, thanks,' I said and as I turned and asked her, 'you're not coming? Oh God.'

'No. Can you smell that? I'll stay here. Keep watch,' she said with a grin. I carry on alone and yes, the smell was bad. It was even worse than being back in that stable with the general. By the time I got up into the jail, I didn't smell practically great but I had managed to get myself in exactly where I needed to be. I crept around still not sure what I was looking for. The jail was a lot emptier than I had expected it to be. In fact, there wasn't anyone in the jail at all. I carry on looking around in till I got to a cell that was heavily guarded and not by the towns or even royal guard and that wasn't right. Whoever it was, was probably someone who really shouldn't have been in there and maybe that's what Blue was talking about. It had to be the master but something didn't feel right. But whoever it was, I'm pretty sure that's what I was looking for. But how to get in there. After a few minutes of thinking, I went back outside to find Liv. She was still waiting for me.

'Wow,' she said, 'great smell.'

'Yes, yes okay. I know I know. I need you to go back to the stable by the east gate. My horse is in there. He's black n white and big. There's also a monkey there called Marley. Get them both ready to travel tonight. On the way, tell Mrs French anything I've told you.' And with that, she was gone. I sat there in the cold smelling water thinking long and hard about who it might have been and how was I going to do this without the queen shooting me on sight. My years of being a general was coming back to me slowly but surely and as the sun was slowly going down in the late afternoon. I made my way back up the tunnel and into the jail once more. I didn't have my sword or my bow but there were only two guards but I couldn't be sure and I needed to be. I very quietly crept around looking for another way into that cell. All the others were empty and none of them joined into the next. I was running out of ideas and time. The longer I was in there, less chance I had of getting out of there. 'Think, think,' I said to myself. Then out of the dark, Marley appeared.

'Need a little help,' he said. I didn't get a chance to answer, as he went running over and past the guards still waving those arms around the prefect little decoy as the two men followed him off but it wasn't that easy. As I went over, the cell door was locked and I still couldn't see who it was inside. Then I heard the monkey coming back my way. I hid and as Marley went past, I jumped out hitting one of the guards to the floor. Just as the other one appeared knocking me into the wall, I turned and punched him once twice. He was bigger than the first one and it had taken me a good few blows to knock him down for good. Marley had the keys from the first one. By the time I had won my fight, we unlocked the door and I went in. Marley waited outside keeping watch. As I walk in there, I couldn't believe my eyes. Blue was indeed right. I knew it as soon as I saw it and it was definitely the bigger surprise of my life. Nikita, the queen and daughter to the emerald king my king, was laying on the cold damp floor of the town's jail. This was definitely not right. She was cold and weak.

'What are you doing here?' she said in a low voice.

'I'm here to rescue you,' I replied, sounding like I knew what I was doing. I've been walking around half expecting her to shoot me and now I'm carrying her out of the town jail.

'What a beautiful woman,' Marley said.

'Lead the way outside,' I replied. I followed the monkey out back to the end of the tunnel. Liv was there waiting for us. It was night by the time we got outside.

'Who is that?' she asked.

'Liv, you don't know who this woman is?' I asked her.

'No, Marko, I don't.'

'Is my horse ready?'

'Horses,' she said. 'I'm coming with you but yes everything's ready. Show me the way back to the stables.' As we made our way back quickly through the dark night, something was definitely not right here. I was carrying the queen following a young girl with a monkey. If someone had told me this two weeks ago, I would have died laughing but this was exactly what was happening to me. Again, far too many questions, as I found one answer there were many more questions. Mrs French was waiting in the stables.

'Oh my,' she said, as soon as she saw the queen, 'where in heavens did you find her? Not the jail surely.' She had answered her own question.

'Yes, that's exactly where I found her,' I replied.

'Here.' She grabbed a blanket wrapping it around a very cold looking woman.

'We need to move,' I snapped, as I helped the queen up onto the horse. 'Marley, ride with Liv,' I said, as I turned and thanked Mrs French again with a hug.

'Take good care of her, Marko.'

'I'll try,' I said, as I jumped up and held the queen close to me.

'Not her,' she replied looking at Olivia.

'You have my word,' I said without question. She smiled and we all left riding hard straight out the stables and from the capital gateway and back into the jungle.

We didn't get far as the panther jumped out at us.

'Stop,' he shouted.

'Kai?' I asked.

'I'm not him,' a familiar voice said.

'Char?'

'Yes, come on. No time. Follow me.' As he jumped off changing direction, we were still in the jungle but heading north as we were going back around the town, my heart didn't feel right. But my head trusted this was the right thing to do. After an hour, we arrived back at a place I'd not long left, May's house. The door was open.

'Go in,' Char said. As I got down to take Nikita inside, Liv followed with the horses. The house was empty and I put Nikita in the chair and got a fire going.

'This will warm you up.' Then Marley came in.

'Please stay and watch her,' I said to him. 'I'm going to look around.'

'Hey, miss, you really are very beautiful,' he said, as he pulled the blanket up and sat with her. Liv also came back and they all sat by the fire. I went back outside. Char had already gone again. I don't know what it was about him but it felt like there was a reason he brought us back here again. I made the bed where I had slept and put Liv and Marley in there to sleep. I sat in the chair next to the fire all night looking at Nikita. The questions oh there were still so many questions. It was all going around and around in my head. All of it. A council member missing, now the capital's queen had been in jail. What the hell was really going on? The next morning, I woke up. I didn't even realise I had fallen asleep.

'Here you go,' Liv said, 'I made tea.'

'Oh, thank you.' I sat up, scratched my head, as I looked around. I jumped up. 'Where is she?'

'Relax,' Liv said, 'the queen is fine. She helped me make the tea. She is just washing herself. Don't worry. Marley's outside in the tree keeping watch. I've got this all under control.' I wasn't sure coming from someone so young but I sat back down and drunk my tea. Then she entered and walked over to the fire. Liv give her a cup.

'Thank you, my darling,' she said.

'No problem,' Liv replied, then went back off.

'Hello, Marko,' she said.

'My lady,' I replied.

'Thank you for rescuing me. I honestly thought the world had forgotten about me,' she said.

'How long have you been in there?' I asked.

77

'I'm not sure months maybe even a year,' she replied. 'How did you know where I was?'

'Blue.'

'Oh good. He must have got my message.'

'No idea if I'm honest. He told me to go to town, get in trouble and go to jail. He didn't tell me you would be in there. I even said to him you of all people would shoot me if you even saw me and now, I'm rescuing you from the capital jail. Nikita, please tell me what the hell's going on.'

'Marko, do you know a witch called Sasha?'

'Oh, not her again. Yes, I've only just recently got into a fight with her and the black shadows.'

'Oh, so you know.'

'I know that the witch and someone called Soren Kane and his gang. The black shadows are all working together and that they have probably kidnap or have even killed the golden master.'

'What?' snapped Nikita. 'So, the plans are already in motion.'

'Plans? What are you talking about, Nikita?' Marko sat down.

'Sasha, the shadows all of that is a front to what is really going on here. You remember Barus?' Again, my heart stopped. My old life really was coming back to hurt me in every way.

'Oh God, Nikita. Please don't tell me he's behind all of this.'

'Not directly, no. Sasha and the darkness are trying to finish what he started all those years ago. They want control of it all. The kingdoms, the council, all of it and all of us are at risk now.'

'What? There's no way the darkness are strong enough to take it all.'

'Marko, you have been gone too long to know the world we live in now. Greed, money, power is all out there. Do you know who sits on my throne in the name of greed?'

'No, Nikita. I don't.'

'My very own brother.'

Silence filled the room. Nikita sat down. I really did have no idea. What the hell has happened to the world in the years I had been on my own but again before I had a chance to even breathe, the door swung open and Liv came running in followed by a very scared looking Marley.

'Black shadows,' she cried out.

'Liv, where's my bow? Marley, take Nikita, hide in the room you stayed in last night. Wait for Liv to come back before locking the door and don't come out.'

'Okay,' the little monkey said, taking the queen by the hand as they went off. Liv came back moments later. She had my bow and all the arrows she could carry and under all of that, my sword.

'You going to need this,' she said, as she put it all down on the chair.

'Thanks,' I said to her. 'Now go up with the others.' She threw her arms around me.

'Be careful.'

'Yes, okay now go on off with ya.' Once they were all inside and the door locked, I just stood by the front entrance door to the house looking, listing and waiting for any sign of trouble. It didn't come at first. I don't think they knew we were there. Then a wolf appeared sniffing the air. He could smell lunch or should I say Marley. Then another one appeared followed by a gang of five or six no make it eight men. I was good with my bow and I was getting better at using my sword again but ten versus just me was a bit of wishful thinking. The first wolf got closer as the other one hung back a bit. It was as if he knew I was there. A couple of the men were not so clever as they carried on coming towards the door. I stood completely still but then I could hear a noise. It was coming from behind me, as I turned around to see the general running straight at me.

'The door,' he said. It was the first time I'd heard him speak in a very long time. I just about got the door open for him in time as he charged straight out only just avoiding the first wolf as he crashed into the first group of men knocking them all over with a massive thud. I shot my bow hitting the first wolf and knocking him down. I shot it again twice. Three times, all my arrows hitting the gang of men as my target but the surprise had gone and the other wolf had managed to grab my horse pinning him to the ground.

I shouted at the top of my voice, 'Noooo, Jessy.' But I couldn't do anything as the other men were now running at me. I managed to shoot another three before they got to me. The rest all fell with a few swings of my sword. It was only the other wolf to go now, as I run up to where he had my horse pinned down. I couldn't let anything happen to him, not now. But in that moment, I forgot the basic rule of combat. I was blinded by my feelings and the wolf turned on me with a grin, grabbing me by my arm as he had me in his mouth biting down hard. The pain and the blood ran out as he swung me around. Finally, he let me go and I went flying into the air and straight into the side of the hill with a massive thud. The pain I was in was much worse than the lion and the blood. I was hurt badly this time but thankfully, the wolf didn't get a chance to finish me or my horse off as Char appeared again just in time and he wasn't alone. Kai and Nina were both with him. The wolf ran for his life as the two panthers and the leopard came running over and all I could do was just laid there dying then nothing.

Chapter 7

New Friends

I wasn't really awake. My eyes were closed and my brain not working as I lay there. I can hear the birds from outside and feel the warm sun on my face. Its warmth was comforting. I wanted to move but I just couldn't. I lay there in my half awaken state. I didn't really know if I'm alive or if I'm dreaming. Then as I open my eyes, it hit me. I was home. I was in my bed. I could hear the birds and feel the sun on my face because I really was in my own bed. A massive grin came over my face. *Oh yes*, I thought. It was only a dream. A big, horrible, nasty dream but within second of believing that and as soon as I tried to move, it all came crashing back down to earth with the pain in my arm and down my body as I looked at all the bandages, the wolf attack. Everything that had happened in the last few weeks hit me like a horse in the head. Yes, I was home but none of it had been a dream at all. I slowly started to move and got up. Then I heard voices. Liv was the first to appear.

'Oh, you're awake. Thank God. It's about time,' she said. 'Come on. Let me help you downstairs. There all have been waiting for you.'

'Who?'

'Come on, come on,' she said again. After a painful few minutes, I made it down the stairs. Nikita, Blue, Nina, Marley and a fit again happy looking May-li were all there.

'May,' I said, 'are you okay?'

'Yes,' she said, as she hugged me a little too tight.

'Oww,' I said.

'Yes, I'm fine. Thanks to Sahara. Are you okay?' she asked.

'Well, I'm still here, so unfortunately yes,' I replied.

'Good job to old friend.' Boom that voice once more.

'Blue,' I said, 'good to see you too.'

'Marko,' Nikita said, 'you saved me twice in one day. How will I ever repay you for this?' I put my hand on her arm and smiled.

'Right. Now you awake, let's get started,' Blue said again in that loud voice of his, as he started going on. May looked at me.

'Marko, you will need to rest here for a couple more days. Then it's time to finish what we started. The master is still missing. The darkness now has full control of the capital. The black shadows are growing with every day that passes. War is coming, my friend, and we need you to be ready.'

'Me? Why me?' I said, still hurting and confused.

Blue stood up. 'Are you not a general in the—'

'No,' I interrupted, 'I am not a general. I haven't been for a long time and don't intend to be any time soon.' With that, I hobbled out the door and out into the meadow. Deep breaths. I thought I really was getting sick of it all. Yes, I got a kick out of the little adventure I had and meeting all the old friends I had truly missed but again here, I was broken, bleeding, hurt. Not Blue not Sahara not Nikita. No, it was me. I was sick the

83

first time of getting hurt for other people and now it was happening again. I walked over to the barn.

'Jessy,' I said.

'Wow, Marko. He lives.'

'Yes, and wow you actually do talk.'

'Well, when you call me by my name, then yes I do, but anyway just because I wasn't talking to you, I've never left your side plus I may not have talked to you but I've been talking to everyone else. Blue, Sahara, May.'

'Oh really?'

'Yes,' he said, 'I'm the only one who keeps you out of trouble.'

'Hey. For a horse, you actually pretty funny. But thanks, old friend.' My horse was indeed called Jessy. He hadn't spoken to me in years because I didn't use his real name. Instead I called him what everyone else had called me for many years, the general. In the beginning, that was my way of not forgetting who I really was but then I did forget and I had got so use to calling him that, that I didn't stop. I just kept on and so he didn't talk to me anymore and yes that is bloody stupid but it's the truth but he was still my horse and a friend. But I did have a few new friends. One of which was outside calling me.

'Marko,' she said.

'Hello, Nina. Can you walk okay?'

'Yes, a bit. Why?'

'Come on. I want to talk to you alone.' We walked down the path a bit.

'You don't really know me,' she said, 'you know that I travel with the master. I don't really know you. I know of you and the service to the emerald king but you came looking for

84

me and with some good friends helping you. You managed to rescue me. I'm guessing you don't really know Nikita but again with some help, you rescued her to and in return, I along with Kai came to help you too. Blue and the other keep telling you they need you but it's not really true. The light in this world comes in many different forms. As long as the light stays true to its self, there will always be light. All the people, the animals both you humans and us magical needed to stay together no matter what. Do you understand what I'm saying?'

'Yes, I think so.'

'Look, you really were a general once. Not just another solider but the general to the emerald king's royal guard. You think just because you've been on your own for a long time, you are not good enough but you know what, Marko, I'm a leopard. I hurt on my own. I live in the jungle on my own. I'm still a killer, a hunter, clever and wise. What do you think you are? Why do you think they all believe in you so much? It's because you are you and you really were the general to the emerald kings. His general to his royal guard. Nothing more nothing less. Why don't you think about that while you here resting.'

Later that afternoon, Kai who had been sitting outside and Nina left, Blue was next.

'Blue,' I said, 'I'll try my best to be ready.'

'I know you will,' he said, then he also left. I sat back in my chair. It really was nice being home but I hadn't had this many visits before Liv was in the barn where we now had three horses. Marley was up on the roof keeping watch. Nikita was down by the river and May was sitting next to me trying her hardest not to kill me.

'Stop moving, you big girl,' she said.

'Well, stop hurting me then.'

'My God, how did you ever survive all them years on your own.'

'Oi, I've never been hurt by a wolf like this before in my whole life.'

'Okay calm down and stop moving,' she shouted. 'I could change you into something if that makes you sit still.' I instantly stopped moving.

'You wouldn't.' I just looked straight at her. I couldn't tell if she was joking or not. 'How's Sahara?' I asked laying back in my chair and finally relaxing.

'Oh, now you stop moving around.' She laughed. 'She is good. She has been a really big help to me. She fixed me up and now I'm doing the same to you. So did you miss me then?'

'Oh yes of course, you would have loved walking down that smelly old water pipe into the jail then getting into a fight with a couple of wolves. It's been the absolute best day of my life. Can't wait for tomorrow.'

'Marko,' she said with a straight face, 'that was four days ago. You have been out cold for four days. We really didn't know if you'd be okay.' I could see the hurt in her eyes.

'I'm okay, May. Promise that's not my point. We are going to war. I'm proud to be on your side.'

'Once more, general.'

'Thank you, captain.' Nikita arrived back in from her walk followed by a tired looking Liv.

'It's getting cold out there,' she said.

'Well then, let's get the fire going and have some food, after dinner.' Liv, Marley and May all went up to bed. Nikita stayed with me downstairs.

'It's my turn to look after you by the fire,' she said.

'Can I ask you something, Nikita?'

'Yes, of course you can,' she replied.

'You know why I left, don't you?'

'Yes, I think so.'

'You know it wasn't because of you or your father or anything to do with the capital.'

'Yes, of course I do.'

'So why do you hate me so much?'

'Marko,' she said with a surprised look, 'I don't hate you. I've never hated you. I loved you like a big brother. My father loved you like a son and I always loved you for the way you did your duty to the king and the capital. We were all heartbroken when you left,' she said. 'Why do you think I hated you?' she asked.

'Nikita, your father sent me to protect Indiana, Sahara's mother.'

'Yes, I know that,' she said.

'But do you know that she made me promise to protect Sahara before she died and I failed with that promise and because of that, the guilt drove me completely mad. Your father told me that with help, I'll get through it but someone else told me that you hated me and that you were going to have me killed. So, I left before that could happen.'

'Who, Marko? Who told you that?'

'Your brother. Do you remember his teacher?'

'Yes. Elba's yeah of course I do.'

'Well, he told me. Nikita didn't say anything else after that and I fell asleep.

The next morning, waking up in my house was great but waking up in my chair was not so.

'Good morning,' Nikita said, 'are you okay?'

'Not really,' I said, 'can you help me up to the bed, please?'

'Okay.' So slowly and painfully, she helped me upstairs.

'Where is everyone?' I asked.

'May and Liv went into town. I don't know where the monkey is.' She laid me out flat on my bed. It felt a lot better. I drifted back off to sleep. Nikita went outside.

'Marley,' she said, 'Marley, can you hear me, silly monkey?' She went into the barn tripping over the chickens.

'Just as I had done. Good morning, miss,' Jessy said.

'Good morning to you. What is your name?'

'Jessy.'

'You have been Marko's horse for a long time, haven't you?' she asked, as she stroked him.

'Yes, miss. I too served your father in the royal guard. He was a great king.'

'Thank you, Jessy. That's very kind,' she replied.

'Miss, what do you want with the monkey?'

'I need to send a message to Largo about my brother.'

'Write it down. I'll go find him for you.' Again, she thanked him and went back into the house. A few days turned into a week. May taught Liv how to ride her horse better, hunt for rabbits, even a little bit on how to use a sword. The general, I mean Jessy, spent it in the barn resting like me. The feeling of home was good. Marley on the other hand the poor little monkey wasn't having such a great time. It was colder and the trees of the foster wasn't as easy as the jungle. I myself got better and stronger every day and not just back to normal. I know now that war was coming and I couldn't avoid it any longer. I practised with my sword and my bow every day. In between that, running for strong legs, digging my garden to work out my back by the end of the week, I felt like a completely different man or maybe a lot like the old general again. As the end of the week arrived, so did a bird. A dove to be precise.

'Look,' May said, as it landed on the fence of my garden with her magic ring on, she managed to catch it. It was carrying a message. 'Marko,' she shouted over. 'It's time,' she said, as she threw the bird back into the air and it flew off. I followed her into the house where Liv and Nikita were sat.

'What is it?'

' Blue needs us to go the council. They are meeting again. They want us all to be there,' May said, 'Liv you ride with me.'

'My lady, are you okay to ride a horse?'

'Yes of course I am,' she snapped, 'a bit too much as we all noticed it.'

'Nikita,' I said, 'it's a full day's ride.'

'I'm fine.'

'Come on, Liv,' May said, 'let's get the horses fed and ready.' As they left, I asked what was all that about.

'You may be the queen, you maybe the daughter of the king that we both served but out here and right, now you are just another person. Stay here if you want to.'

'Marko please,' she said, 'it's not that I have no problem riding a horse.'

'Well what then, is there something you're not telling me?'

'It's what you said about Elba's the other night. He was just a teacher but now looking back, I'm not sure if he was actually a wizard and that he could have been hiding his magic and controlling my brother. It all makes sense. He told you to go, he told me that you abounded your post and then after that, the darkness started to take over in the capital. My father was so old by then and with you not around, he could be the other half of Sasha's dark plans. I know my brother has nothing to do with this.'

'Nikita, you need to tell all of this to the council tomorrow. They need to hear it from you, okay?' May and Liv came back in.

'Everything okay?' May asked.

'Yes,' I said, 'Liv come and help me upstairs, please.' I left the two women alone.

'May,' Nikita said, 'I would like to thank you. We've never really spoken before but I know who you were in the royal guard second in common only to Marko. You both have honour and should be very proud of yourself in the way you served my father.'

'Thank you, my lady,' May said, as she nodded her head.

As we left the house behind again, May and Liv rode out in front. Star looked amazing in the morning sunshine. Nikita rode Liv's brown horse in the middle and me and my old friend, Jessy, were at the back along with a very scared looking monkey.

'What a bunch we were.' It didn't take long before we were joined by another one as Kai was waiting for us. May didn't stop. She just carried on. He joined the back of the group and we all just carried on and on. Then before long, Nina joined in as she ran out in front of us. It must have been a great sight to see from afar.

It had taken us nearly the whole day as we rode on through the middle kingdom from where my house was. It was nice just ridding. There really were a few parts to this world that I hadn't actually seen before. I wasn't sure if May or Nina was leading the way, but I guessed that we were going back to the mountains where I had met the council before and Sahara's home, Thorberg. I didn't know how I got there the first time. Thanks to Largo knocking me off my horse. It was very late afternoon as the mountains came into view but what a view it was. Nina still leading the way as we made our way up into the mountain path. We soon spotted a few guards who showed themselves to us. I wasn't sure what they were hiding here in the mountain but as the door way came into view, I was shocked. It really was something to behold. We entered and followed the path up a bit higher. It was darker at first before it opened up and I got to see it from the outside for the first time, there was a whole town inside the mountain. Even though I had been there before, I had no idea how long it had been there or anything about this place. I did feel safe and I could also feel that Sahara was close by. I couldn't explain it. I didn't know how or why I could feel her. This place had a mystery about it. As we got closer to the main town, the guards escorted us in. Kai and Nina went on a head, as the rest of us had to stop and wait before a man in uniform walked up to us.

'I'm Nikolas. I'm captain here at Thorberg,' he said, 'and as you can appreciate when the council meets, we take the upmost precaution for everyone's safety. Let me show you to your rooms before the meeting goes ahead,' he said, as we followed him along. Liv was with May which made me feel better. I had told May all about meeting Mrs French in the market and who this young girl was and how she helped back in the jail. But she was still only a young girl. But as May knew all about Mrs French, I knew Liv would be safe with her. Unfortunately, that meant I had to carry on putting up with

Marley. It was good having him around. I just wish he learnt to shut up as he couldn't sit still and even when he was talking, he still waved his arms around but it was nice having him there. A while later, the guard knocked on the door.

'Are you ready, sir?' he asked.

'Yes,' I called out. 'Come on, Marley. It's time to go,' I said, as he jumped on and we left the room. I followed the guard as we walked in to where I had to meet the council. Beforehand, I could see Blue, Kai and Nina all sitting together. Around one-half of a big stone table, Largo was once again laying in the top half of the hallway. He was so big he didn't really have much choice. May and Nikita were on the other side. I walked in and sat in the empty chair next to Sahara. I sat and listened to them all talking. I wasn't really concentrating. There was something wrong but I just couldn't work out what it was. Then Sahara hit me.

'Oi, what is it?' she asked.

'Nothing,' I replied. Blue was explaining how the black shadows had been getting bigger by the day and were coursing more and more trouble, as they moved from town to town and were even getting closer to his home in the north. Sasha had a plan and she knew what she was doing.

'All right,' Blue said, 'there's something different about her.'

'No one from the darkness has ever been in control like this before,' Kai added.

'And it's not just men she gathering either,' Nina said.

'No,' Blue replied, 'dark witches and wizard from all over. Plus, the animals from the forest, wolves, lions and we also now believe it be true, Whistleroot has returned.'

'Can I ask what's the capital doing about this?' Nikita asked as she stood up. Since she had been in the jail, she didn't know much about what was going on.

'Nothing,' Largo replied. She looked shocked with the news and sat back down again. She didn't look very happy but no one around the table did. I stood up.

'Largo,' I said, 'with everyone looking at me and I can feel it too, how are we going to fight both the darkness? And the capital? You are all very powerful and the council to this world I understand that but we are not an army,' I said pointing to everyone, 'and you all know the army of the capital. The same army I was leader of once. The king's own guards number in the thousands.'

'No, we are not,' he said, 'but we don't need one either, general.' He had never called me that before "ever". 'You and May along with your pet.' I wasn't sure if he meant the girl or the monkey but it didn't matter. We were taking both, I thought to myself; *'need to carry on looking for the master'*. Blue and Kai, carry on gathering all and any of our allies from the jungle. We will need all the help we can get. Captain Nikolas,' Largo said who had been standing at the back of the room this whole time, 'how many men do you have?'

'Two hundred here but we have 650 in all, sir,' he replied.

'That's good. Nikita, you can stay here with us. You will be safe here,' Largo said. 'When the time is right, you will be queen once more.' After the meeting was over, Sahara and me walked for a while.

'Are you okay?' she asked.

'Yeah, I'm getting better. Thanks to May. Whatever you did to her seemed to have worked.' She just gave me that smile again as we walked on.

'Marko, I'm not talking about your wounds from the wolf. You did a great job fighting the shadows, saving the queen from the capital, all of it. That is exactly why me and Blue need you back. We need you to be the leader. We all know you are to lead this fight for us but you need to be okay with it. You need to be focused, and are you?' she asked.

'Sahara,' I stopped and looked at her and held her hand she was still so beautiful. I couldn't help it any longer. I loved her too much. 'I'm back,' I said. 'Sahara, I'm really back. The guy you all need me to be, the general and yeah, I'm okay with it all but I will always carry the guilt around from that day. You understand that, don't you? The feeling of failure and that I wasn't good enough to protect you let alone the king.'

'Marko,' she snapped, 'you did your best. You saved me. It was her choice to go back and there's nothing you could have done. Indiana, my mother, gave her life to save Largo. I have never blamed you for that and I never will,' she said, as she put her arms around me and held me tight. It was the first time in 20 years that I felt her, held her that close to me. The love was real and I could feel it. After Sahara had left me on my own, May caught up with me.

'Hey,' she said, 'so what the plan then, general?' she said with a big grin and laughed.

'Don't be funny, captain,' laughing myself.

'Who would have thought me and you were going to be like this once more, May,' I said.

'Oh, come on, Marko. It's not that bad.'

'Not yet,' I replied still smiling. 'May, I still need you to take the lead here. I'm still learning about this world again. I have no idea what I'm doing or where to even start looking for this wizard. We were lucky finding Mimi in that cave and we had help finding Nina like we did.'

'Look,' she said. 'We were a team then and we are again now.'

So, I stopped and with a fun filled look on my face, I said, 'Captain?'

'Yes,' she said with that smile and a salute.

'Make ready, we depart first thing in the morning.'

'Yes, general, right away,' she said walking off laughing to herself. It was good to joke around with her again. I trusted her with my life completely and when the time comes, I wouldn't want anyone else but her by my side.

The next morning came and we were all ready to go. Blue was giving May some instructions, as I stood there with Jessy all ready for another adventure.

'My old friend?' I asked him.

'This time, we in this together,' he replied. Then Nikita came over to me.

'If there's any chance that you could try and save my brother, will you?' she said.

'Yes, of course I will, Nikita. I don't know how deep he's into this but if I can, I will.'

'Thank you,' she said, then it was Sahara's turn.

'Marko, I trust you and May I have done and will always do.'

'The same as you two trust me and Blue?'

'Yes of course we do, why would you say that, Sahara?'

'Because,' she said, 'you can't trust anyone else outside of that circle.' She looked at me deeply. I knew that look. I wasn't sure what she was trying to tell me but it was enough for me to listen to her.

'Okay,' I said, 'I understand.'

'Good,' she replied, 'because I mean it. Things are moving here that even I'm not sure about, so please be very careful.'

'Okay,' I said again. She hugged me again very tight but it felt different this time. May looked over. Even she noticed and gave me a look. Things were getting bad.

We all left Thorberg behind. As we went on our way back down the mountain path, Liv rode ahead with May as I got stuck with Marley. It wasn't long before we were back in the grasslands of the middle kingdom. The sun again felt good on me as we were now in early spring. The few days being back at home then seeing Sahara again made me feel more comfortable. My mind was still troubled by all the questions. Some we had answered some we hadn't and some we just didn't know if they were true or not but like I had told Sahara, I was me again. I was ready and forced on the job in hand, or so I thought.

'Come on,' May said, 'you're lagging behind again.'

'Where we going?' I asked.

'Well,' she said, 'we going to see a man about a dog…' I really had no idea if she was joking or not. There was a town up ahead called Weir. A friend of Buka lives there and I'm hoping he might be able to help us.

'Okay,' I said, as we rode on into this town which wasn't the biggest in the world. 'I had been here before a very long time ago and I remember it being bigger,' I said to May. She just laughed at me. 'Maybe because you were a kid back then,' she replied.

'Oh yes, maybe you're right.'

Chapter 8

The Journey

We arrived at the inn which was in the middle of the town.

'He is inside sitting in the corner like normal,' she said. 'Liv, my dear, stay here with the horses. Keep watch.'

'Yes, miss,' she said. Marley jumped up on to the roof and out of sight.

'May, when I said take the lead, I didn't mean take over.' She didn't reply. We walked in and the place went completely silent. As everyone looked around at us, we just stood there then. From the back of the room came a massive laughing sound.

'May,' a voice shouted out.

'Watch out,' she whispered to me. Then from out of the shadows, came this huge man who had no hair, was almost as tall as Blue and had the biggest arms I've ever seen on a man.

'This,' May said, 'is Harden.'

'May-li, wow it's great to see you again, my dear.'

'Cut the crap, Harden. I'm here to see the boss,' she said.

'Oh, May, that's too bad. The poor guy passed away last year.

'Maybe,' she said, as she turned and laughed, 'Buka said you'd say that.' As she pulled out her ring and picked the guy straight up into the air, the look of shock on his face as brilliant as he was flowing around in mid-air.

'Put me down,' he shouted with a please on the end.

'Where's the boss, Harden,' she snapped at him.

'Okay, okay I'll take you to him. Please just put me down now.' And with a thud, he landed back down on his bum. We all left the inn and walked over the road to a small house. Marley watched from the rooftops.

'Come in,' Harden said to us. As we entered the room, it was only small and there was only a dog sitting by the fire and a couple of chairs. 'Sit down,' he said to us as he just stood there.

'So where is he then?' I snapped at the big guy. May looked at me with that shout up sort of face.

'Please,' she said quickly, 'don't let my friend bother you.' I turned and looked at her, as the dog moved.

'It's okay, May,' he said.

'Hang on, you mean we here to actually see a dog?'

'Yes,' she said looking at me. 'This is the major. The tracker. I told you about him years ago.'

'What? The one you always banged on about how great he was, he's actually a dog?'

'Yes, I am,' he said putting his nose in my face. 'What is it to ya?'

'Major,' May said in her calming voice, 'please this is the general. We both really need your help?'

'Oh, do you now and with what?' major asked.

'You're the only one I know who could help us find the golden master. Blue told me to find you.'

'Hmm good old Blue at it again I see. Getting everyone else to do his dirty work.'

I knew that feeling. Blue had done the same to us to but no I trusted Blue and I wasn't going to listen to this.

'Excuse me, major, we are asking for your help. If you're not interested, then just say so we got a long way to go.'

'Tell me,' he said, 'what's happened to the master?'

May look at him. 'He's been missing for weeks now. Mimi was attacked in the temple and Nina too.'

'Okay, okay. I owe Blue a favour so if it's time then it's time. Hay,' he asked, 'get the waggon ready. We going for a ride.' Harden left for a few minutes then he came back.

'All ready, boss,' he said. We all went outside. The major hoped in the back of the waggon and got comfortable as Harden rode up front. May walked over to her horse and pulled out a piece of cloth.

'Liv darling, come and sit in here. It'll be more comfortable for you,' she said, as they walked over to the waggon.

'You don't mind, do you?' May asked.

'No,' the major replied. 'I love kids.'

'This was the master,' she said, 'I'll leave it for you to get a good smell of.'

'Thanks,' he said. Then just as soon as we had got there, we were all gone again. After leaving the town behind, we followed the waggon a little way before it stopped again.

'May,' the major called out, 'I'm picking something out but it's very faint.'

'Okay what way?'

'Unfortunately, it was south.'

'Oh,' she said.

I didn't like the sound of that. 'What up?' I asked her.

'It's south,' she said, 'and you know what that means.'

'Oh God please no. He surely can't be in the capital. We were just there and he definitely wasn't in the jail.'

'Marko, he's not going to be and you know how big the place is but with major sniffing him out, we find him for sure this time,' she said again.

'Well, we can't go back to your house again.'

'No, straight in this time. We can't delay any more, Marko. We need to get him back now.'

'Okay let's get this finished then.'

The capital was going to be a long way. The morning had turned into late afternoon and we were losing the light.

'May, we're going to need to stop soon,' I shouted over to her.

'Yeah, I know,' she replied.

'But where?' I asked. We all stopped.

'Where are we?' Liv asked.

'We in the middle kingdom. There's not much out here. Major, could you lead us to the river?' May asked.

'We could find somewhere a bit safer along the river.'

'Then follow it right back into the capital?'

'Yeah,' he said, 'I can smell it. It's not that far.' An hour ride and we were there right by the river. We made camp and got the horses sorted. May and Liv got the fire going as I went and caught us some dinner. It was late by the time we were all settled. I sat there thinking it had been another day and still nothing.

The next morning started badly. It was cold and raining and the path along the river was very slow going in the wet mud and before we knew it, the morning soon turned to the afternoon. It seemed like we really weren't getting anywhere. Then as we came up to a top of a hill, the capital came into view. We could see it all laid out in front of us just like it had been for me. Weeks beforehand though I'm wasn't sure exactly how long it had been as it was all such a blur. There was an old barn just down the hill and where we could all finally get out of the rain. There was more than enough room of the waggon and all the horses. As we got dried and comfortable, May noticed the major standing over by the door.

'What it is?' she asked him.

'We have to make a plan,' he said. 'I can definitely smell that the master is close by now.'

'Okay,' May said again, 'so, Harden, why don't you take the major down there and find out exactly where he was.'

'But I had another idea.'

'What?' she said.

'You can't do that.'

'Why not?' I replied.

'Because she's a kid.'

'Look, May, you weren't there. Mrs French got Liv to help me for a reason. She knows the capital better than anyone I've ever met before. She knows every ally, every rooftop and every turn plus who's going to be looking for a kid and their dog running around the place.'

'I can do it,' Liv chipped in.

'There you go,' I said.

'And she'll be safe with me,' major said. 'You take Marley with you.'

'By the way, Marley,' I shouted out. 'Where is that monkey?' I said, as I got up and walked over to see this wet hairy mess sitting there looking all sorry for itself.

'Hey, I've got a job for you, my friend,' I asked.

'Oh really,' he replied, 'and what is that?'

'I need you to go back into the capital with Liv.'

'You did say you never been there before and now twice in a week. Oh, how exciting,' he said in the most unexciting way possible.

'Come on, Marley. I'm trusting you to keep an eye on her.'

'Okay, okay yes, yes,' he said again.

'We go in tonight,' I said, as I walked off back to the others. 'May, you and me will go down there with them and find a place out the way. Then Liv and major can go out in the morning. Harden, you stay here with the waggon.' Night soon fell and me, May, Liv and the dog left for the capital under the cover of darkness. It didn't take us long and before we knew it, we were all in the stables on the northern gate. Liv wanted to go out right away instead of waiting for morning. May wasn't sure but as all was quiet, I agreed.

Marley followed on over the rooftops as Liv and major ran around from street to street me and May had no choice but to sit and wait for them to return. Major with that noise of his to the ground walked on as Liv followed on. They walked around for nearly an hour and were almost in the middle of the capital by the time they did. Major stopped dead in his tracks.

'What's wrong, Liv?' asked his close.

He replied, 'I can smell it in the air.'

'We've come a long way from the others,' Liv said, 'shall we go back to them?'

'No,' the dog said. Onwards as they kept going, they soon came out on to the main street and he stopped again.

'There,' he said. Liv looked up to see a very big and well-lit square building. 'We need Marko to see this,' major said.

'I'll go get him,' Liv said, as she ran off. Marley followed on from up high as major went back and sat in the side ally way and waited.

Marley had trouble keeping up with Liv. At first, the monkey was going from rooftop to rooftop as Liv ducked in and out of the street turning here and turning there, then nothing. Marley heard a strange thud and then voices. As he slowly came down, he could see Liv laying on the ground. She had managed to run straight into one of the guards and had knocked herself out. Marley keeping his self out of the way just watched as the guards laughed.

'What a stupid girl,' one of them said.

'Well, what's she doing running around so late.'

'Not my problem,' the first one said back to the other. 'Come on, it's not worth the hassle.' After a few minutes, they carried on their way. Marley jumped down to check on her.

'Liv,' he said. Olivia said nothing. She really was out of it, so he did the best to drag her out of the way before carrying on his way back to find Marko.

It was very early morning. As Marley arrived back to the stable, May was sleeping and I was standing in the doorway as Marley came crashing in out from the dark, he was out of breath and shaken.

'What's wrong, Buddy?' I said. He tried talking but couldn't breath as he was waving his arms around again like he always did. It woke May up.

'What's going on,' she asked, 'where is Liv?'

'And the major?' As he was still out of breath, he was trying to tell us but just couldn't. May got hold of him.

'Calm down,' she said, 'calm down.' After a few minutes, he was okay.

'Major has found him,' he said. 'Yes, yes, found the wizard he has.'

'That's great,' I said, 'where is he? Let's go.'

May also said, 'No.'

'No, no,' Marley said. 'One thing at a time. The girl first wizard second.'

'What's happened to her?' May asked.

'Well, come on, come on,' he said, as he rushed out the door. We all left the stables. Marley pointed the way back to where he had left Liv laying on the ground. She was still out of it when we found her. I pick her up and Marley led us all the way back to where the major had been waiting for us in the alleyway. He had been laying out the way this whole time.

I put Liv down as major asked, 'What happened to her?'

'She ran straight into some guards,' Marley said.

'She'll be okay,' May said, just as I looked around to see the start of one of the ends to the royal palace.

'Please, major, don't tell me his in there of all places.'

'Yep,' he said.

'You have got to be joking,' I replied, as I stood there looking at it. 'May you know full way we're not getting in there anytime soon.' She looked around and I could tell she was thinking about something. We had both been royal guards long enough to know there's no back door. The walls were all straight up and thick stone, so not easy to climb and every entrance was double guarded. May was still thinking.

'Major, you sure he definitely in there, right?'

'Yes,' he said.

'And you can tell exactly where from here?'

'No, but I could if I was in there.' She walked over to Marley.

'If I can get you in there, could you find him without getting caught?'

'Yes, yes,' he said, 'I'll be okay. I think.'

'May,' I asked, 'how are you going to get the monkey in there?'

'Have you ever seen a monkey fly before?' I didn't get a chance to answer. She pulled out her ring and made Marley float right up and over the wall. The look on his face was pretty funny. He landed with a thud on the roof and not on my head this time. He gave us a little wave then he was gone. I picked Liv up again and we all made our way back to the stables. The light of the morning sun was just coming up as we got back to the barn where Harden was still waiting get some rest.

'You all look pretty tired, I'll take care of Liv,' he said, as we all slept out the morning.

Chapter 9

The Golden Master

It was early afternoon. By the time I woke up, May was up as the dog was still snoring but most importantly, Liv was awake. I got up walked over to her.

'Hey, young lady, how are you feeling now?' I asked.

'Yes,' she said with a smile. 'I'm okay, thanks. That was a first for me running into a guard like that,' she said. I smiled back.

'Well, just as long as you all right, you are a part of our group now and I promised Mrs French I would look after you.'

'Where's Marley?' she asked.

'We left him in the palace.'

'Oh,' she said even she knew that wasn't the best place for a monkey to be. As we sat around talking in the barn, Marley was making his way around the royal palace talking to himself.

'Marley, do this, Marley, do that,' he mattered away, as he made his way along from rooftop to rooftop and in and out of windows and towers. He lived in the jungle so knew who the master was and of course climbing was second nature to him. But unfortunately, being out on the rooftop in the midday sun in the south meant it was hot and unlike the jungle where it's full of trees for him to hide under, the palace rooftops were very hot. Indeed, he needed a rest and ducked into a room high up in one of the towers. There wasn't anything inside so Marley just sat on the window ledge and cooled off. It wasn't long before he heard voices. As two guards walked in, he just managed to get back outside before they noticed him. The guards dragged in an old man and dumped him on the floor. When Marley heard that they had gone again, he jumped back into the room. There laying on the floor was the golden master. He was hurt and very weak. Marley ran over to him. *What luck*, he thought.

'I can't believe I've found you,' he said to the master.

'Marley,' came a very weak sounding voice, 'is that you?' he said.

'Yes, yes,' said the little monkey. 'We need to get out of here, yes back to Blue,' he said again.

'No, Marley,' the master said, 'my time had finally come. I'm too weak now to leave here,' the old man said. Marley wasn't sure what he meant and he didn't hang around as he jumped back out the window. Back in the barn, it was mid-afternoon. May suggested we get ready and head back down into the capital.

'Major, stay here with Liv and look after her. The rest of us will go this time,' I asked.
'Yes of course I will, general,' he replied back. We left the barn behind and as we made our way back down into the capital once more. Harden pointed, 'Look over there. Smoke,' he said, 'and a lot of it too. It's coming from the palace,' he said again. Me and May looked at each other and both said "Marley" at the same time. We rode on hard down the hill and

straight in and didn't stop until we were right back by the palace and where we had left that monkey.

'I hope he's all right,' I said to May. The palace building was indeed on fire. There were people and guards everywhere. The commotion was the perfect way for us to get into the palace. Harden stayed with the horses as me and May ran in through the gates. We both knew our way around the place as it hadn't changed much in 20 years and it wasn't long before we found him.

'You see, you see,' he said all excited.

'Yeah we saw you set the royal palace on fire. Come on.'

'Come on,' he said running off, 'this way.' We followed him and before long, we were at the doorway to the room where he had seen the master. 'In there,' he said, 'yes, yes in there.' We could see there were only the two guards which wasn't going to be a problem. I said to May, 'But there will be more. We need to be quick and get out of here.'

She said, 'Okay.'

'You ready?' I asked her. She just smiled back at me. A few minutes later, we came crashing through the door and indeed laying there on the cold floor was the golden master. May rushed over to where he was laying. She picked him up into her arms.

'May-li,' the old man said in a very weak voice. 'Is that really you?' he asked.

'Yeah, I'm here, master,' she replied. 'I've finally found you again, my master,' she said through the tears.

'May it's you,' he said, 'I need it to be you.'

I didn't understand what he meant by that but she did. 'I've taught you a lot and I can see you are finally wearing the ring.'

'Don't talk,' she said, 'you are too weak. We going to get you out of here,' she said to him.

'No, May, you are stronger than you know. Believe in that and you can be the witch they need you to be,' he said. She didn't say a word. Then the master gave May an old piece of string that he was wearing around his neck. 'Give this to Sahara. She will know what to do,' he said with his last breath and with that, the old man fell away.

May was heartbroken and even I was in shock at what just happened. We had finally found the wizard we had been searching for all this time and just like that, he was gone for good. I put my coat over the old man's body. 'Come on, May, we need to get out of here and back to Thorberg as soon as possible.'

'We can't leave him,' she cried. I knew she was right but we were running out of time. I put my sword away and picked up the wizard. Marley led the way out as I looked at May. 'You ready for this?' We both knew we had to fight our way out of this. We followed the monkey through the palace down stairs and along hallways, bumping into people with every turn. May was behind me as we reached the outside courtyard but there was guards everywhere. Harden rode in with the horses just in time and I just managed to get the master on to Harden's horse.

'Get back to barn and the get waggon ready,' I told him just as we had some unwanted attention and the guards were finally on to us but as the palace was still partly on fire, it gave us the edge. Without even thinking about it, I drew my sword and rushed into battle. I tried to give May enough time to get to her horse and make a run of it. 'Go,' I shouted over to her, 'get the master back to Sahara.' She didn't look back as she got to the gateway and made it back out into the streets of the capital. I was a bit busy fighting and didn't really know how I was going to get out of this. Then Jessy came running knocking two guards over but as I tried to fight off the last one, I was knocked over and fell down some steps. I wasn't hurt but it was enough to open up the wound from the wolf attack. As I sat there, Jessy finally got to me.

'Need a ride?' he said. I just smiled but as I got on, I felt the blood again. We made a run for the gates but just as we were nearly there, Jessy was hit by an arrow right in the back leg. He jumped up and nearly threw me right off at the same time but we made it through the gates and on through the capital and back up the hill. We got back to the barn where Harden had the waggon all ready. The master was all covered up in the back with the dog and Liv sat in the front.

'Marko,' May said, 'Jessy hurt really bad and there was a lot of blood.'

'Yeah, they got me,' Jessy said, as May jumped off her horse and came over to look.

'Hold still, old boy. This is going to hurt,' she said to him and yes, it did as she tried to pull the arrow out.

'Harden, you better get going back to Thorberg. We'll catch up.'

'Okay, if you sure,' he said.

'Yeah, get going,' May said. He didn't need telling twice and they left. It had taken us a good few minutes to patch up Jessy's leg.

'Marko, you really need to be careful,' May said. 'I'm not sure I got it all out. You really shouldn't be riding him too far with that leg. It's cut pretty deep.'

'I'm okay,' Jessy said.

'You sure, old friend? I can't lose you as well. Not now. You started talking to me again.'

'I'm fine now, are we going or not?' he replied.

'Come on then. We need to move,' I said just as we heard horses approaching. 'Now let's go,' I shouted out. Jessy bolted off and May wasn't far behind us but unfortunately, we didn't get very far as Jessy began to slow down.

'You okay?' I asked him.

'No,' he said. He was clearly hurt and in pain. 'May, go on get the others back safe. I'll draw them off. Lay low and I'll be back in a few days.'

She didn't answer. She wasn't going to admit it but she knew I was right. She left and followed the waggon. I got off, picked up my bow, my sword and all my arrows I had.

'Jessy,' I said, 'keep going as fast as you can down that pathway but be careful not to hurt that leg. I'll follow on behind. I might be able to pick a few of them off. You'll be lighter without me.' He nodded and went off on his way.

The pathway was darkened over by trees on both sides. The perfect place for an ambush. There were ten rides following Jessy but my arm started hurting again. They had no idea I was there. As they all passed by me, I shot the last one off. I ran along the tree line changing sides as I shot another one clean off his horse. I had a job keeping up with them but then I managed to shoot another one down but by then, they had gone. I had to grab one of the horses, drew my sword and give chase. By that time, they had noticed and stopped up ahead. There was only six left. I charged straight at them, swiping my sword around. I got another one and then another but I didn't notice one coming at me from behind. He knocked me straight off the horse and sent me crashing to the ground and right onto the side that was already hurt first from the lion and then my arm from the wolf and those steps back in the capital. It was very painful and knocked the wind out of me but I had done enough as the last three made a run for it. I just about manage to pick myself up and with my bow in one hand I collected up enough arrows before getting back onto the new horse. I rode off to find Jessy. He wasn't in a good way. By the time I caught up with him, there was more blood and he could barely walk.

'Come on, old friend,' I said to him. 'We have to keep moving slowly.' As we made our way back to the river and back northwards and away from the capital, all was quiet. Unfortunately, we weren't getting anywhere. Jessy's leg was bleeding and I was in pain from the full. My arms were also bleeding and my rigs were hurting. I had to stop so I tied up the house, got Jessy into the river to wash his leg then found him a nice place to rest. I got a little fire going and kept watch as late afternoon had turned into night. As I sat there, me and my horse were both hurt and bleeding but again all was quiet.

Chapter 10

Hurt and Alone

After the meeting at Thorberg, me and May had left with a girl and a monkey. We had since found a man and his dog outside. Our little group looked like the weirdest bunch but we all had a job to do and we all knew it. Blue, Kai and Nina made their way back to the jungle. Largo had told them to go and gather our allies but I wasn't sure what he had meant or who he had meant but if Blue was involved, then it was going to be interesting. The three of them arrived back at the temple. Mimi had been there the whole time and was now fully recovered from the fight she had been in.

'Good morning,' she said to them with a siss as Blue. Kai and Nina walked in to greet the snake with a bale. Then they all sat and spoke about who they wanted or needed to find and how they were going to get them all to fight. Normally when the council member comes calling, you do as you're told but this wasn't just a favour. They were asking them to go to war. As they spoke, a group of six big male gorillas turn up.

'Good,' Blue said, 'my brothers are here to help.' Kai looked at Blue.

'That's a good start, Blue, but it won't be enough.'

'We're going to need the elephants,' Nina said.

'Yes, you are right, my love,' Kai said. As the three of them sat there planning, May and the others had been riding back to Sahara at Thorberg. They weren't being followed but May didn't want them to start as they pushed on all through the afternoon and into the late evening before they had to stop and camp out for the night. At first light, they were off again and it was late afternoon again by the time the mountains came into view. They all felt a big relief that they had made it back in one pace. Kai and Nina left Blue at the temple. The leopard like Mimi had now recovered from her injuries as they made the way through the jungle quickly and quietly. They knew where the elephants would be this time of the morning. The jungle had a massive herd of elephants with many bulls, females and their calves. The leader of the group was a female called Luna and her mate was called Rajesh. Now on this sunny morning, Kai knew the elephant family would be at the dust clearing. This was a dry strip of sand just off the river. The elephants loved rolling around the mud and sand first thing in the morning. Rajesh and the other males would take it in turns looking out while the females and calves played in the mud and sand. When Kai and Nina turned up, they were greeted with a laugh.

'Oh, so the panther's back. What do you want now or are you here to congratulate us on a job. Well done back in that town.'

'Good morning, Rajesh,' Kai said, 'and yes that's exactly what I wanted to do. Can't thank you enough,' he said giving Nina a little wink as Rajesh stood very tall and proud. 'I come to you this morning to ask you another favour.'

He was just saying this as he was interrupted. 'Oh no you don't,' shouted a voice as Luna walked over. 'Don't come here thinking you can order us elephants around every time you need help with something.'

'Please, Luna,' Kai tried to say.

'No, I'm not having it.'

'Largo,' Nina stepped in and interrupted. They all looked at her. 'Sorry, my love,' Nina said to Kai, 'but we've not got time for this. Luna, Rajesh, Largo has sent us here. He needs the pair of you to come to the temple. Blue is there waiting.' The pair of elephants looked at each other. They knew they couldn't get out of this.

'Come this evening,' and with that, Kai and Nina left the elephant family in peace. Back at the temple, Blue, the other gorillas and Mimi were all waiting. As Kai retuned, he told Blue all about the elephants.

'That's good,' Blue replied. 'But where is Nina?' he asked.

'She's gone off in to the jungle to look for the water buffalo. We need as many as can get,' Kai said.

'Yeah, I agree,' Blue replied.

'How do you think Marko's getting on?' Kai asked Blue.

'I'm not really sure but we need to keep the faith in our two young friends. Marko and May were good together once before and we need that again here and now,' Blue replied.

'Don't worry,' he said again, 'old friend. It's not them I'm worried about.'

'What do you mean?' Kai asked.

'It's Largo. He's not telling us something I can feel it but I'm not sure what it is.' Kai looked at him.

'Funny there's something that don't feel right in all of this like his gathering us all together for a reason and war with the darkness, isn't it?'

'Look,' Kai said still a little confused, 'you trust Largo, right?'

'Yes, of course,' Blue said.

'Then stop worrying about something you can't control.' Blue didn't reply.

It had been a few days since we had escaped the capital. Me and Jessy weren't in a good way, both still hurt and bleeding. It had been slow going and we were still nowhere near the mountains. It was raining and I was wet, cold and tired but I couldn't risk Jessy going any faster with his leg the way it was. I had to walk as even my extra weight was too much. Luckily, we had the other horse to carry the stuff that Jessy couldn't. As we made our way north along the river, I was worried and I just couldn't risk us stopping. The threat of the black shadows was too much. It was only a matter of time before we bumped into unwanted company. I was in no fit state to start another fight. Another morning turned into late afternoon and the again into the evening. We were going so slowly that I didn't want us to stop and I had filled my mind with the thought of Sahara as a way of stopping the worry. It wasn't ideal as it gave me something else to worry about. What she said about trust, that wasn't right. What was she suggesting? That I couldn't trust. Largo or anyone else I really didn't like all these questions. As we carried on, the rain had stopped and the late evening sun came out just long enough of me to easy my troubled mind. I didn't really know where I was but I had no choice. I had to keep going. The sun soon went again, as it was now dark and very cold. The pathway along the river was very wet and hard going. I had to stop. I got the horse tied up and a fire going. I felt unwell and I sat down. I fell straight to sleep in the cold, wet mud. May and the others had finally made it back to Thorberg. Sahara and Nikolas, the captain met the tired looking travels.

'New friends, I see,' Sahara said. As she walked up to greet May, she could only manage a smile. 'I do hope you are all okay,' she said again.

'We will be,' May replied. 'Any news on Marko? Is he here yet?' she asked.

'Oh.' Sahara looked shocked. 'No, he's not come back since you left together.'

'We got separated after we left the capital,' May said again.

'What news on the master?' Sahara asked. May didn't answer as she just give her the string that the master had given to her and as she looked over to the waggon Harden had the body covered, blanket in his arms. Sahara looked at May. She put her hand on her arm.

'It's okay. He's at peace now, May, and truly with the spirits exactly where he wanted to be. You know that more than anyone.' May could only manage a smile. 'Rest now, all of you. Rest here in comfort and tomorrow I'll send the captain and his man out in search of Marko. Come, captain, we have much to talk about.' The witch and the captain walked off to the main hall where Largo was waiting.

'Send out your best man,' she told him.

'Yes, first thing in the morning,' he said.

'He must be found, yes,' Nickolas said, 'but it's a massive area and could take weeks?'

'Search the grasslands and back to his house first,' she told him, 'I'll put word out to everyone.' Sahara sounded worried. The captain just looked on. He knew what had to be done and left her alone.

'So,' Largo said to the witch, 'have they found the master?'

'Yes, but it's as we thought. He's gone.'

'Hmmm,' the dragon said after a few minutes of silence. 'So do you think she is ready for this, Sahara?' he asked. 'Is she really the one you want?'

'Yes, I believe so,' she replied, 'and so did the master.'

'Okay then. I'll go to the temple and talk to Blue then when I return, we make all the arrangements.'

First light the next morning, Nickolas and his men all left ridding from the mountains down into the middle kingdoms in search of the missing general. Which wasn't soon enough as that very same morning, Marko was still lying face down in the wet mud. Although the sun was out and the rain had stopped, Marko was in no fit state to move any more. Fever had set in and time wasn't on his side. Jessy on the other hand his leg hadn't gotten any worse. The captain and his men were soon ridding through the grasslands. After an hour, they had all split and been given their orders. It was a massive area to cover and in search of just one man. A whole day later and still nothing, two of the man went to Marko's home and after tripping over the chicken, left with no general in sight.

'Marko,' Jessy said with a knock to the head but no answer at first. After a few seconds, he still got nothing even for a horse. Jessy was smart enough to know he had to do something to help his master out of this. Then after another go, Marko woke up.

'Hey, old friend,' he said in a very tried voice. Jessy managed to untie himself and walk over to where Marko was laying. He helped him up slowly and onto the other horse and the pair carried on up the path northwards. After a few miles, Marko told him to change direction and head for the sand kingdom. Jessy looked at him.

'Are you sure?' he asked. Marko didn't answer and they carried on. Jessy knew exactly where he wanted to go but it wasn't going to be easy.

The afternoon had again turned into the evening. As the horses got their first touch of sand under their hoofs and warm it was too, the sand kingdom was nothing but sand and it was a very hot place for the horses to be riding into. Luckily, it was evening and that was the best way to get through it was by ridding at night. Jessy still couldn't go very fast and it was some hours later before he finally found it. Jessy turned to Marko. 'Look,' he said, 'Nava.' But Marko was again out of it and barely holding on. Jessy pulled on the other horse. 'Come on,' he said, as they carried on over the last few sand dunes and then down to the oasis.

Nava was a little town built around a small lake in the middle of the desert and was home to another one of Marko's "friends". Captain Nickolas and his man had been searching for another full day trying to find the general but he soon realised it wasn't going.

'Well, there was just no sign of him anywhere,' the men all told their captain. He told them to look for another day if still nothing to go back. The captain himself retuned to see Sahara. Jessy led them down to Nava where one of the old guards was living. He knew like May did only too well that there weren't many of them left now. But Marko needed help from someone who was out of the way and Cassian was exactly that person. As they rode into the little town, they were met by a dark stranger dressed all in black. Their faces were covered and straight away, Jessy thought it was Sasha, the dark witch.

'Who are you?' shouted the person to Marko in the dark night. They obviously couldn't see he was not with it. 'Who are you spoke, the horse?' No answer. It was like they were a bit confused for a second then another voice from behind.

'Jessy, is that you?' As Cassian walked out from the dark behind him, Jessy shaking his head all excited.

'Thank God I've found you,' he said, 'quick, it's Marko. He's hurt badly.'

'Marko,' came another voice from the stranger who had been standing in front of them, Alexis was Cassian's twin sister and she as well as Cassian had served with May and the general in the king guard for many years. She walked forward and the pair of them helped Marko get down from the horse. They dragged him into their little tent. Cassian put both the horses in their stable, gave them food and water and patched up Jessy's bad leg. The horse told Cassian everything right from the start and up to how they came to Nava. Alexis got Marko undressed out of his still wet and muddy clothes and attended to him.

'Marko,' she said, 'what have you been getting yourself into now?' No answer, as he just lay there completely out cold. After an hour, Cassian walked back in.

'How is he?' he asked.

'Not good,' his sister replied. 'He's been in some sort of fight. This looks like a bear or lion. Something bad and he's covered in bruises. It looks very bad and not to mention the fact that he was wet and covered in mud which is why he's feverish. How the hell did he managed to get out here?'

'Jessy,' Cassian replied, 'who has got half an arrow stuck in his leg and who has been bleeding a lot.'

'I thought the pair of them were living a simple life out in the middle of nowhere.'

'They did but Sahara asked Largo to find him and that the golden master is dead.' Capital Nickolas arrived back at Thorberg and reported straight to the witch as he walked in, she stood upright.

'Any news?'

'No,' he said, 'nothing. There's absolutely no sign for him anywhere.' Just then, May walked in and heard what he had said.

'You must keep looking,' she snapped at him.

'May,' Sahara said, 'calm down. We will but we both know what Marko's like. It's probably a good thing we've not found him. Carry on the search for another day,' she told him.

'Yes, my lady,' he said and left.

'Where is he, May?' Sahara asked. 'He hasn't gone home and he's not anywhere that the guards have looked.' May walked around the room and thought to herself for a few minutes.

'There a few places he could be. We still have a few old friends who live out of the way, but I can't be sure!' she said.

'Do you think you can find him?' Sahara asked her.

'Yes, I'll leave right away,' May replied, as she walked out and into the count yard, leaving the witch sitting by herself. It was her turn to worry about Marko. Truth was she thought about him a lot. It had been so long ago since her mother. She had ignored her feelings for top long and now it may be too late to tell him the truth. Liv and Marley were with the major as May walked up to them.

'Any news?' the major asked.

'No,' she said, 'but I'm going out to look for him now.'

'I'm coming too,' the little girl said without even hesitation.

'No, Liv, sorry darling not this time,' May said.

'I need you to stay here and look after Marley. I don't want him getting into trouble.'

'Hey,' the monkey said which did make Liv laugh a little.

'Come on,' she said, as the pair walked off to where Nikita was sitting.

'Harden, I need your help. Will you come with me?' she asked. 'I have to find Marko and quick.'

'Yes of course,' he said.

'Then get the waggon ready. We may need it. Major please watch over Liv for me. Won't be too long I hope.'

'Yes, miss,' the dog replied, 'you have my word.' And with that, the two got ready and headed out. The next morning in Nava, Marko woke up. He could hardly move and he didn't know where he was or how he got there. He felt pretty rubbish and in a lot of pain. Then Cassian entered.

'Morning, general,' he said, 'it's been a long time.' Marko looked up at him and smiled.

'Cassian,' he replied, 'my friend. Thank God it's you. Though I'm not sure it's a good morning.'

'I don't suppose it is for you, general. How are you feeling?' Cassian asked.

'Yeah great,' Marko said, 'I'm ready for another adventure.' As he laughed, Marko's face told a completely different story. 'Well, talking of adventure, Jessy the poor old boy with the arrow stuck in him has been telling me about the one you having at the moment dragons, pirates, witches and the jungle all within weeks.'

'Wow, my friend, you don't hang around, do you?' Cassian said laughing at Marko who could do nothing but lay there not seeing the funny side of it. 'We had honestly thought you had gone off to live a quite boring life on your own in the woods.'

'Look,' Marko said, 'I did. My life was all of that nice and quiet until Largo dragged me back into this life.' He sounded upset, broken almost.

'Okay, okay,' Cassian said, 'calm down. Whatever it is, we will help you like we have always done, general.' Just then, Alexis walked in.

'What's going on in here, Cassian? Stop it,' she said, 'he needs to rest go and check on the horse,' she told him.

After another full day of searching, the captain and all his men retuned back to Thorberg, Nikita, the queen, was still sitting talking to Liv in the courtyard about the capital and how they both missed their home. Nikita may have been queen but talking to this young girl about their city and listening to her talk about Mrs French, the market and the other children she helps was very nice indeed. The guards all rush in through the gates. It shocked Liv with all the noise and she looked worried as the little girl was. May followed by Harden in the waggon had gone all the way back to the barn where then had been just outside of the capital and the last place they had seen Marko from there they found the road where they had split up on and then a trail of the body including a lot of blood. They followed it on for a couple of miles before coming across where Marko had made camp.

'May,' Harden said, 'look there's been a body here laying in the wet mud and blood. There's a pool of blood over there to which must have been from the horse were and Marko must have slept here.'

'He can't be in a good way if he spent the night in the cold, wet mud,' May said to Harden. May found some more hoof prints and blood. 'They must be going northwards. Come on, we can't be far behind them,' as they followed the track north. Marko was still laying on the floor as he felt pretty rubbish. Alexis sat with him.

'So, the master really is dead?' she asked him.

'Yes, me and May found him in the palace. He was weak and he had been missing for weeks which is why I started this and left me home in the first place.'

'Oh really,' she said to him.

Sasha had her plans in play. The master was only the beginning and with the shadows growing by the day, there wasn't much she couldn't do plus now that Whistleroot was back, she was loving it and more power hungry than ever before. Blue's home was still her next target and with him being busy with the council, he was going to be in for a very big shock. But not one of us knew what her plans were. The council were playing catch up and that wasn't good.

Kane with some help from Sasha and of course Nikita's brother was now fully in control of the capital. No one knew it and the city went on like it always did with the ships in the harbour coming and going and the market place as busy as ever, plus people from all over the kingdoms come in and out like never before all seem normal but then maybe a little bit to normal. Sasha arrived in the palace and Kane was there to meet her. He told her about what had happened and about the fire and that the master had gone. He couldn't tell her if he was still alive or not but Sasha wasn't that bothered.

'It was minor setback,' she said to him, 'no matter the bear is on his way up to the north. Now let's see how they deal with this part of my plan.' Kane looked at her first.

'The leopard, now the master, they are on to us,' he said.

'So what?' she shouted back at him in that temper. 'Good. I want a fight. They are no match for me now. None of you are,' she said again as she laughed and walked off. Kane knew he had to watch his back and not just from the council but from Sasha and that bear.

Chapter 11

The Code

Luna and Rajesh along with Mimi the snake, Blue, Kai and Nina were all at the temple along with the other gorillas, the buffalo and a few others. They were all waiting for Largo to come and as like with me in that first market town, they all heard him before they could see him. The temple was big but not even Largo could fit inside. He landed in the clearing right outside the front of it and was greeted by everyone.

'Hello, my friends,' he said, 'you all know me and why I come to you now with grave news. The golden master has been taken from us and you all know what that means. The time has come once again for all of us to fight. The darkness has declared war on the council and its supporters by attacking this very temple and killing a council member. We need to come together now and stop this once and for all. The darkness is growing and people are getting hurt.' Mimi looked upset at the news of the master. The elephants looked unsettled and all the other monkeys were chatting and jumping around in the trees. Everyone expect Largo was on edge. Blue BOOMED with that voice again.

'Please, everyone,' he said, 'this is no joke. None of you want to go to war but you all know what has to be done. Our world can't fall into darkness not now not ever.' Mimi rose up again like she did before.

'I will fight,' she sissed.

'So will we,' Nina and Kai both said standing together.

'So will we,' Luna said standing tall with Rajesh by her side. The other gorillas beat the floor with their fists and the buffalo nodded.

'Go spend the word through the jungle and to the capital and beyond,' Largo said, 'if war is coming, we all need to be ready, each and every one of us.' After the meeting, Largo sat and spoke to Blue.

'We have something else to talk about,' he said.

'Yes,' asked Blue, 'what is it?'

'Me and you are very old, my friend. We have been in this fight for far too long. The master knew all too well what we were getting into and now our friend has gone. Sahara wants this girl to join the council in the master's place.'

'Yes,' Blue said. 'He did train her and she was his favourite,' replied Blue.

'Yes, but I'm not sure she ready for this, Blue,' Largo said. 'She not been a witch long enough for what we asking for and time is not on our side here.' Blue thought about it for a few minutes.

'Largo,' he said, 'there's never going to be a good time for this or an easy answer. You know only too well replacing a council member had never been an easy thing to do. We had the same talk when Sahara replaced her mother, Indiana.'

'Yes, you are right, old friend,' Largo said to Blue, 'if you and Sahara believe in this young girl, then I have no reason not to believe in her as well.'

'Largo, you know as well as I do what she did for the king all those years ago and the support to this very council. She has shown us all loyalty and has always followed the code.' Largo still wasn't sure but he agreed.

'I will leave it up to the pair of you to get her ready for this.'

'As you wish,' Blue replied. As Blue was about to walk off, Largo had something else to say.

'Marko never came back with the others. He's been missing now for a couple of days.' Blue turned and looked at Kai.

'I'll go,' Nina said, 'I'll leave right away.' And with that, the leopard was gone.

An hour later, Harden stopped the waggon.

'Look,' he said, 'the bloody trail changes direction.' May thought for a second. She had no idea why Marko would not be heading back to them at Thorberg and it made her worry even more.

'What do we do?' Harden asked.

'We keep following the trail. We have to find him and quick.' Alexis was still on the floor next to Marko.

'Why would you put yourself through this?' she asked him.

'Because you know full well what the code said.'

'Yes, I'm a supporter to the council. The same as you and my brother and May. We all served you in the king's guard and we all know what the code said. But why have you put yourself through this? You have done your duty. You own the council nothing and I'm sure you of all people could have said no to that.' Marko didn't answer for a minute. He didn't need to. Alexis knew exactly why. 'Marko, you have been avoiding this from the very first moment you met her and I only know this because I was right there with you when you met her, remember?' Again, no answer.

'You can lie to yourself all you want to about what you've done but you're the one laying here hurt. You're the one who needs to tell her the truth because we may not be able to save you again.'

Nina ran and ran through the jungle and into the grasslands. There was no law to say the animals of the jungle had to stay in the jungle but different parts of the world had their own damages and for different reason but she didn't care. She had a job to do. Blue had made it very clear that Marko needed to be found and quick. She had a great sense of smell but even for her, this wasn't going to be easy. Largo had said he left the capital and would have been heading north on his way back to Thorberg, so she had a good guess where to start. Another morning had turned into the late afternoon. As May and Harden reached the edge of the sand kingdom, the trail of blood had stopped and she still had no idea where he could be. They made camp, got a fire going and as they both sat there talking, the sun set on another day. May looked confused as Harden asked her where she thought Marko could be? He didn't really get an answer.

'Well,' he said, 'you have the oasis town of Nava. It's not very big and I don't know it very well or you have the camel traders who live in the caves to the deep south but that's a very long way or the biggest settlement I know of in the desert is Havana to the north of here. May didn't know anyone in any of those places and thought it was strange of Marko to be going that way. The next morning, Alexis and Cassian were both up and out as Marko was still laid out on the floor.

Cassian was washing Jessy in the lake, as his leg was feeling much better.

'Jessy, does anyone know where you are?' he asked.

'No,' the horse said, 'we were supposed to be going back to Thorberg but Marko was in such a bad way and he knew you were here.' Cassian thought for a moment.

'We going to have to get him ready to move then,' he said. 'Can you show us the way back?' he asked again.

'Yeah, of course I can,' he said very proudly.

'Okay we get ready and leave right away.'

Nina had crossed the river and was well away from the jungle now as she went northward, but she had to stop dead in her track. She could smell men and lots of them. She jumped up into a tree and sat very still. Then just as she thought a group of about 20 men walked past, they all looked armed and very dangerous but they weren't alone. With them was a very big and nasty looking black bear. She gasped when she saw that it was Whistleroot. Everyone knew whom he was with that thick, black fur and metal armour. She hadn't seen him in years. Once they had all passed, she sat there in the tree. She didn't know what to do. She had to find Marko but Blue needed to know that it was indeed true. Not only had Whistleroot returned, but he was now involved with the black shadows as well. Cassian got Marko up and ready to travel. He could only just sit on the horse that he had got from the guards but it meant that Jessy was completely free of any weight to walk on. Alexis led the way as Cassian helped. Marko followed on. They all left the oasis behind as they started the long walk back to the mountains. It was easy to go back to the grasslands than walk the whole way through the sand. It had taken them a couple of hours before the green valley's came into view.

May still didn't know where to go and even she knew crossing the sand kingdom in the wrong direction could be so costly. But as they got everything ready to move, they too heard men approaching. Harden looked at her but it was too late to get away as the two of them were rushed by a small group of men. May couldn't reach her sword as she was grabbed. Harden, as big as he was, tried his hardest to put up a fight and knocked one guy into the other. He used the waggon to get in the way as he grabbed his stuff from the back and swung it around. He put up a really good fight giving May time to draw her sword from her horse. By then, they were surrounded but they weren't about to give in just yet.

'You ready?' she asked Harden.

'Yes, why not,' he replied. She looked at him and the fight was back on. Nina jumped down out of the tree and carried on northward until she too came across the same blood and hoof prints that May had found early in the day. By the smell, she knew it was Marko's, so she carried on with no time to lose. She ran on following the scent of it and within minutes, she ran straight into May and Harden who were fighting off the last of the gang that had attacked them. Moments beforehand, the sight of Nina running in was enough to put the last of them off and the three of them were all saved once more.

'Am I glad to see you,' May turned and said to the leopard. She smiled.

'Glad to be of some help, but I think you had this one,' she said back to the witch.

'What are you doing so far out of the jungle?' Harden asked.

'The same as you,' she replied, 'looking for Marko. Blue told me to help find him.' She was just saying as she paused, the three all them all turned around to see horses in the distance. It was Cassian, Alexis and indeed Marko.

Nikita's brother walked straight into the hall where Kane had been talking to Sasha.

'What's going on?' he demanded. Kane really wanted to punch him but he knew now wasn't the time.

'Jasper, everything going according to plan. You are king now just as you wanted and just as Sasha promised that you would be.'

'No,' he interrupted, 'my sister is still out there and so is the council.' Kane really wasn't interested in what this spoilt little brat had to say or who was king. His only interest was in the money and plenty of it. Kane might have been head of the black shadows but again like most part of the darkness, he was only interested in himself. He had a very large farmhouse in the desert on the outskirts of Havana that no one knew about. It was full of gold and jewels from all the years of robbing. He tried to go back there as much as he could but his time had come and he knew it, he had to go away for good. Helping Sasha was his way of paying for that new life alone with his three wives. Whistleroot and the large group of men he was with were heading north. They had their orders and the second part of Sasha's plan was to go after Blue's family in the northern mountains. The master was the first and the easiest because everyone knew where the temple was. Blue was next because Sasha had found out he lived in the north. She didn't know exactly where but she had a good guess and as Whistleroot was from the north, he would be the best one to trick it down. Largo didn't have a home so the only way to get him out in the open was to go after one of his friends. The exact same way Barus did the first time when he went after Indiana. The only difference in what Sasha had planned is that the queen had been replaced with her horrible, little brother who was so desperate to become king he would have done anything she wanted.

Blue was still at the temple with the others. Largo had left as he sat there thinking about Marko. He knew they needed him as well as May, and as many as they could muster but none of them still didn't know if there was going to be a full out war or not and it was that what worried him the most. Kai came over.

'The animals from the jungle are with you, my friend.'

Blue smiled back. 'That's good,' he said.

'What's the matter, old friend?' Kai asked.

'There's too much uncertainty here. The master has gone which leaves the council weak. The queen is been outed from the capital. Marko the one person who we wanted to help us is not the old general I thought he was. How are we going to fight an enemy that just seems to be two steps in front of us and we don't even know it.' Whistleroot and the group of men he was with, had arrived in the northern forest. He knew it only too well. The handpicked group of men he was with weren't like the normal group of poachers that Blue knew. They were well-trained and knew how to go unnoticed. They started on the west side of the forest and moved though without leaving a single leaf out of place. Harden rode the waggon north. Marko and May were in the back as Cassian and his sister, Alexis, along with Jessy and Star rode on behind. The small group finally arrived back at Thorberg by nightfall. Sahara was sitting in her study as the captain came in and gave her the news. She felt a massive sigh of relief, as she walked out to greet the group. She also got a shock when she saw Cassian and Alexis both standing there.

'My lady,' they said, as they both greeted her. She smiled at them.

'It's very nice seeing you both once more,' she replied. 'Marko's very lucky to have such great friends.'

'Sahara,' Alexis said, 'Marko told us everything and we are in. We will honour the code.'

'Whatever you need,' Cassian interrupted his sister.

'Thank you,' she said again before turning to May, as she was just getting out of the waggon. 'He's not in a good way,' she said to her.

'He's here now. It's all that matters.'

Mrs French was sitting in her little house in the market place thinking about Marko and the queen and most importantly Olivia. She hoped the young girl would be all right. As much as she trusted Marko and May and even the queen, she had let the little girl go off with them and it did worry her. Apart from that, Mrs French had her own problems. The capital itself was not a nice place to be in at the moment. Jasper "the king" had announced that the queen had died and that he was now the rightful king of all the earth. Kane and his men were everywhere and they were watching everyone. Sahara, May, Nikita, Cassian and his sister were all sitting around the table where I first met the council. Nikita was desperate to get back in or at least find out what was happening in the capital and with her brother. Sahara wasn't sure that going anywhere near the capital was a good idea.

'Nikita, we all know that you are the rightful queen and when we the council are completely sure and we are ready, then you will be queen again but I will not risk you going back there until then.' Nikita knew only too well from her father that Sahara was right on this one. The fact that the darkness seemed to be ahead in this was not good and they needed to know so they all agreed to let May, along with Cassian and Alexis, go back to the capital.

'You must be careful,' Sahara told May. ' Find out what you can, then come back here. A couple of days should do it.' May agreed.

The three of them well and a half, as Liv was with them, all left the next morning. Harden and the major also left as the dog told May that he wanted to go and see Blue at the temple. All that was left from their little group now was Marley as the little monkey sat on the end of Marko's bed watching and waiting for his friend to wake up. Sahara was sitting in a chair right next to Marko's bed. She knew he'd be okay but still looked worry. Marko had been the general to the king. He was honourable and strong. A leader and a fighter but that was such a long time ago. He was now lying in bed with claw and bite marks from both the lion and the wolf not to mention the bruises from the fighting plus sleeping face down in the cold wet mud for a night meant he really wasn't in a good way. All those years for being out there living the easy life had made him weak and fat and lazy and Sahara knew it would take him a lot longer to recover this time and it was time that wasn't on their side.

Chapter 12

The Fight

Harden along with his friend, the major who was sitting in the back of his waggon, rode east across the middle kingdom towards the jungle where Blue was. The major needed to get to him but the road east was going to lead them very close to the castle that Sasha had been living in and they didn't even know it. They were walking straight into a trap. Sasha was indeed in the castle. At the same time, not only her but the small army she had been collecting were all there too. Men, witches and a lot more others. She had Kane and some of his men in the capital. She had Whistleroot and his men searched the mountains for Blue's home. All the different parts of her plan were now in full motion and the council didn't have a clue about half of it. Largo flew up high into the mountains right to the very highest snow-covered peaks. It was a place only he would go; only he knew about. At the top, there was an opening and he went in. Crawling around the dark cave and dropping down into a massive hole inside was the true home of the dragons. There were only six left. Not that anyone else knew that as Largo was the only one that lived outside in the world. The time had come of Largo to ask for their help. Now as much as he was big and the leader to the council that was his choice. The other dragons chose to live a different life away from the world and in their cave. Largo knew that not all of them would help him but as he already had one on his side, just one more would have to be enough.

'Hello, my brothers,' he said to the group as he entered.

Yas, the female who was with them in the market place the day he found me, walked up and greeted him first.

'Largo,' she whispered.'

'Hello, my love,' he said back to her.

'Largo,' another one said, 'why have you returned to us now?'

Largo turned around. 'Sitka, I'm here to ask all of you for your help. I am one of six left in this world but I remember when we numbered in the hundreds,' he said walking around, 'the darkness has yet again declared war on this world and I will be there to fight it like I have always done. But this time, I'm asking that we the dragons stand together for one last time to show the world that together we are stronger. That the light rules and will always rule and that there's no place for the darkness ever again.' Yas looked at him very proudly. Sitka didn't answer. Then the youngest dragon in the group walked forward.

'I will come and fight with you,' Jedda said. He was smaller than Largo, a brownie colour and a good flyer but most importantly, a fire breather.

'Thank you,' Largo said to him. After a few more minutes, the three dragons left their mountain cave. The east road from where Thorberg was to the jungle was long and slow going. The dog slept out the mid-afternoon in the back of the waggon as Harden plodding along Harden was a big man and had been friends with May, Captain Tai and Buka for years. He wasn't a supporter to the council or its code but even he knew what this could turn into and what side he was on. They went on for a few more hours before stopping for the night. They were out in the middle of nowhere in the middle kingdom, or so they thought. That same afternoon, Blue, Kai, Mimi and some of the other animals were all at the temple. Kai was getting worried, as Nina had not come back. He had just got her back now she was gone again. Just then, Mimi came sliding in.

'Blue,' she siss at him. 'Come quick.' Kai and Blue followed her out of the temple and a little while out into the jungle, a young female gorilla came. Violet was there laying on the ground. She was hurt, bleeding and looked very scared.

'What are you doing here, Violet,' he asked, 'and what happened to you?'

'Blue,' she replied, 'the village has gone. It's all gone.' She was really upset. She spoke through the tears.

'What do mean gone?' he said back to her. The worry on his face and in his voice was clear to see.

'We were attacked late last night, by a group of men—' She was just this saying when Blue interrupted her.

'Who, Violet? Who?' he said again.

The fear on her face when she said his name. 'Whistleroot.' Blue's face dropped and even Kai looked scared.

'So, it's true then. He has returned,' Blue said.

'If that bear's working with Sasha, then we are all in trouble,' Kai added.

'We didn't stand a chance,' she said again. 'They killed all the people and burned all the bridges and the huts,' she said again looking scared. Blue turned around.

'Kai, you and Mimi please help her back to the temple and look after her. I'm going home,' he said and with that, he let out a mighty roar as he beat his cheat then ran off into the jungle. Blue's gorilla brother who had been at the temple heard his call and followed on. The group headed northwards and didn't stop until they got back to what was left of their home.

May and the others had spent the day riding south to the capital. It seemed like May didn't really do anything else at the moment. As from the moment Marko had walked into the inn she had been at, until now, she spent the whole time travelling around the kingdom but she wasn't silly. She knew exactly why and what needed to be done. Going back to the capital was risky and she knew that but she hadn't got there yet as they all had to stop. The middle kingdom was so big and well spread out. There were hundreds of little towns and odd settlements dotted around and one of those was on fire.

'Look,' Cassian pointed over to May.

'Black shadows,' she said, 'and not just a couple either.'

'Fifty maybe,' Alexis added.

'What do we do?' asked Cassian.

'We need to help them,' Liv chipped in. She had almost forgotten about the little girl on the back of her horse. She was one of the reasons they were going back to the capital not that May had told her that. After standing there for a while looking on, they had to move on. May and the twins both knew they were no match. Three vs fifty just didn't work even if May was a witch but the other problem was that within a few miles, there was more men and the same a few miles after that, Cassian stopped.

'This is silly, May. We only halfway there and sooner or later, we going to get into a fight. They're just too well spread out.' She knew he was right.

'Any ideas then?' she asked him.

'Let's go east along the boulder with the desert,' Alexis said.

'That's what I was going to say,' Cassian interrupted her.

'Even in a war, you two can still find time to argue,' May said to them both with a smile. 'But okay, Alexis lead the way,' she said smiling at her brother. Night had followed again in the world. Harden and the major were in the middle kingdom to the north. May and the others were headed east. Blue and his brothers were on the way back north to their home. Kai was at the temple in the jungle with Mimi and Marko was still unconscious with Marley at the end of his bed. Sahara was still there by his side. She looked after him as best she could and her magic was a great help. She was still worried about him. The love that she had for him was real now and she just wanted to tell him that. After a few more hours and as Sahara attended to his bandages, Marko woke up and grabbed her by the hand.

'Sahara,' he said.

Jasper along with Kane was in the capital. Sasha was in her castle and Whistleroot was on his way back to her. He was very happy with how easy it was to burn down the village and how it would hurt Blue. The only bad thing was that Blue wasn't there himself. That bear wanted him, wanted to fight the wizard, the council member. They were the same size almost and the fact that Blue was a wizard didn't bother him in the slightest but he didn't get his choice this time. May and the twins along with Liv were walking back near to where

May's house was. Part of her wanted to go back and see it but now wasn't the time. It was late as the capital came into view but they had made it without being seen. They entered through the northeast gate and carried on walking in a bit further.

'Oh, it's good to be back,' Liv said. Cassian looked at his sister. They had not been in the capital since the king had die and back then, the four of them had all been in the king's guard. Together they all stopped.

'Where we going then?' he asked May. She didn't get chance to answer.

'Mrs French,' Liv interrupted her.

'Yes, Liv,' May said, 'we're going to see her.'

'Okay.' The little girl's face lit up as she smiled. The three of them put their horses in the stables and the little girl showed them the way through the streets but something was different. The place felt different even from when she was there a few weeks beforehand. It had only taken them a little while before they were back in the market place and headed straight to where Mrs French's little house was. Liv knocked on the door and there was no answer. She knocked again a little louder but again nothing.

'Now what?' Alexis said.

Liv smiled. 'Don't worry. You're in my town now,' she cheekily said and ran off around the corner. Within minutes, the door swung open and the little girl was standing in the doorway. The three of them walked in. The place was a complete mess. Liv found a candle and Cassian got the fire started. They tidied up a bit before Liv, May and Alexis went up to bed. Cassian kept watch but being back here in the place didn't feel right and he didn't like it one bit.

The next morning, the sun was up and out early as the sky was blood red in the morning mist. Whistleroot had been on his way back to Sasha when he and the group of men he was with came across a sleeping dog and next to him, Harden. They attacked the pair and Harden was no match to the men let alone the bear. After that, Harden's body was dragged back to the witch's castle and dumped in the cellar. The major only just managed to get away. The same blood red sky lit up. The sky above the northern mountains where Blue had arrived back to find what was left of his burning village. There were bodies of the people and Blue's gorilla family laying around that didn't get the chance to escape. It was not a good sight for everyone to see. Blue was old and had seen his share for war and death but this was personal. He knew exactly who did this and why the anger he felt. The anger all the gorillas felt after seeing it was too much. Blue told his brothers that he was going to stay and search the forest for anyone who may have got out of there and told them to go back to the temple.

'Kai will need you and I'll be back with you soon.' They left their home behind and went back through the jungle back to the temple. The dragons were also on their way down to the temple. Largo needed to know who and how many they had on their side. Yas and Jedda flow around and around over the jungle and over the grassland of the middle kingdoms. The world again could see the pair and the news spend far and wide that that dragons had retuned. Largo wanted to know what was going on so the pair flew from place to place looking, searching. Largo had arrived at the temple where Kai had told him about Violet, the gorilla, and what had happened to Blue's home and who it was that attacked them.

'That bear has returned then,' Largo said to the panther.

'Yes, it looks like it.'

Hmm, Largo thought for a second. The odds were stacking up on them and Largo knew even with two extra dragons, they just didn't have the numbers. Alexis came down the stairs to take watch. Her brother went up to rest. She to saw the blood red sky outside and knew that it wasn't a good sign. She also noticed that there were a lot of people outside. She woke May up come.

'See,' she said to her.

Liv also woke up. 'What's going on?' she asked.

'I'm not sure,' Alexis replied the little girl. The three for them went downstairs. There were a lot of people outside but it wasn't market day. The little girl said to them, 'Look.'

May said, 'They look like Kane's men to me.'

And indeed, they were and they were everywhere out causing trouble, picking on the good people and just all round doing whatever they wouldn't. After Marko left with the queen, Sasha made Jasper king and with that, she had finally taken control of the capital. Kane had made sure that Jasper did as he was told. Anyone loyal to the queen was rounded up and put into the city jail. It was full not like it was when Marko found the queen and that is exactly where Mrs French was alone with a lot more.

'Marko,' cried out the little monkey. He was so happy when he heard Marko speak and now, he was awake. 'Yes, yes, he's awake,' Marley said waving his arms around like he always did. Sahara looked at him with a smile as to say calm down. Marley got the message and left the room. She tried to help him up a bit.

'Where am I?' he asked her.

'You're safe, Marko. You're back at Thorberg.'

143

'Where's May?' he asked again.

'Marko,' she said to him, 'stop. You're safe, she's safe.' She sort of half lied to him. 'Stop worrying. You've been on quite the adventure,' she said to him. 'Do you remember any of that?' she asked him, but he didn't really answer her. He looked tired and confused as he tried getting out of bed. 'What are you doing? You can't,' she told him but Marko was interested.

'Sahara, where's May?' he asked her again. She knew well enough now she'd gone to the capital.

'She has gone with Liv and the twins and where did you find them by the way?' she had to ask him.

'I might have been on my own but I'm not stupid. I know a lot more than you think, Sahara.' He sounded angry with her and she didn't know why.

'Marko,' she snapped back at him. 'What the hell is wrong with you?' Deep down she knew exactly what was wrong with him. Here he was again broken and hurt, not her, not Blue but Marko. She tried to help him back into bed. Just then, the captain walked in.

'Can I help my lady?' he asked.

'Yes,' she looked at him, 'make sure he stays there.' And with that, she walked straight off. The bear and the witch were in her castle. She was so happy with how her plans were going.

'The capital is finally mine,' she told him. 'The master gone and now that monkey's home has gone too.' She laughed. 'Again, the council is weak and light in the world is fading. She was beside herself and very arrogant. The bear just stood there. He didn't care how much fun she was having.

'What do you want me to do with the pirate I found nearby? Eat him?' he said.

She instantly stopped laughing. 'No, you fool,' she told him. He didn't like that. 'Go; take all the men down to the capital. I want all our army there. No one can stop us now.'

'What about the dragons that have been spotted flying around?'

'What about them?' she snapped at him. 'It's no matter. They're no match for me now,' she said to him again laughing. The power had gone to her head and she was completely mad now. Again, the bear really didn't care for her or her power. He would eat her just the same as he would anyone else. The only reason Whistleroot had come back was because he wanted to fight Blue in between eating anyone or anything that got in his way. Yas and Jedda arrived back at the temple where Largo and Kai were.

'What news, my friends?' he asked them.

'Largo,' she said, 'there a big group of men heading for the capital.'

'How many?' he asked.

'Several hundred,' she said, 'plus there are a couple of smaller groups spread throughout the middle kingdom and the capital now has a new king.' Largo looked shocked.

'What?' Kia said.

'A thousand men,' he said.

'Not all men,' Jedda said, 'witches and animals plus that bear was leading them.'

'We're out of time,' Largo said, 'we can't let them reach the capital. Send the word out. We met them in the lower valley.'

'Largo, where's Nina? We need her.'

'I don't know yet but I need you to go now,' he told the panther. So, Kai left with the elephant herd plus the water buffalo.

'Yas,' Largo said, 'I need you to fly back to Thorberg.' And told her how to get there she left at once. Kane knew the bear and the army of the darkness was on its way. His men had done a good job of filling up the jail so he knew there'd be no resistance from inside the capital or so he thought. He had no idea that May and the twins were back plus not forgetting the one person who knew the city better than anyone else a little girl called Olivia. The three of them were still locked inside Mrs French's little house in the market place.

'Let me go out there,' the little girl asked. May looked at her.

'No, Liv. I'm not risking you going out there.'

'Oh, come on,' she said, 'you know how well I know this place. I'll be out and back before you know it.' Alexis turned and side to May.

'She may be right, May. We can't risk getting stuck in here but we can't risk being caught either and we're not getting anywhere being stuck in here.' May thought for a while and had no choice but to agree.

'I'll go with her. No one know me here,' she said, so the pair left right away. Captain Nickolas stood there watching as Marko tried his best to get out of bed even if he wasn't getting anywhere.

'So, you really were a general in the emerald king royal guard?' he asked.

'Yeah, I was,' Marko answered.

'How the hell did you manage to go from that to this then?' As he pointed to Marko who was now sitting up in the bed. Marko didn't like his tone. Nickolas knew the story and the reason why he left but still the captain was pushing his luck.

'Look, captain,' Marko said, 'are you going to help me up or not?' He didn't answer. He just walked off. Marley then came back in. 'Oh good. I need you to help me, my little friend.

'Me? Yes, yes of course,' he said.

'Go out and find Jessy. Tell him we leaving. Make sure my sword and my bow are on the horse, Marley.'

'Yes, yes don't worry. I'm on it,' he said, as he was already walking off out the doorway. Marko had no idea where she was but they brought him here to lead and that was exactly what he was going to do. The dragon Yas arrived at Thorberg. She landed in the same hall as Largo had been in before Sahara walked in.

'My lady,' the dragon said to her.

'Are you Largo's mate?' the witch asked her.

'I am,' she answered, 'he has sent me here to tell you the bear is leading their army down to the capital. He sent a panther and the other animals to try and stop them.'

'That's madness,' a voice said from the back, as Marko came stumbling through the doorway and down to the table. 'Why would Largo send half our army into that battle knowing full well they're outnumbered?'

'He doesn't want them reaching the capital,' she said to him.

'Sahara, you told me you needed me to lead you to be the general you once knew. Here I am now. I'm ordering you, dragon; go back to Largo. Tell him to call it off. We are stronger together. Tell him Westmoor. Now go.' She didn't need telling twice and flew up high into the mountain and out into the afternoon sky. Marko looked at Sahara.

'You are a witch, are you not?'

'Yes, you know I am.'

'So, you know I'm right. Blue and Nina are both missing. May and the twins are where exactly. Liv, Harden and the dog gone. Kai is heading straight into trouble and the only men we have are all here doing nothing.' The anger in his voice worried her. She had not seen him like this before. 'You, Blue and Largo are all what has left of the earth council. A council that protects and defends. So why are you not doing any of that? The darkness has blinded us from the very start. Sahara, tell your captain I want all the men fully armed and ready to travel.' She loved hearing him say her name but not like this not here not now. She was almost crying by the time he finished and left her alone. Captain Nickolas was walking straight towards Marko as he left her alone.

'She wants to talk to you. Get everyone ready. We leaving here,' he told him, as Marko walked off.

'To where?' the captain shouted at him.

'Westmoor.'

Westmoor as a little town in the northeast part of the middle kingdom. It has a very big but unfortunately very old fort. It was a place where the emerald king used to base his troops in time of war, and it was the perfect place for Marko to start being Marko.

The major had trouble getting back to the temple. He was hurt and very tired but he knew where he was and he knew where he could go to rest up. A few miles later, he was walking through the meadow and up the path to Marko's little house. Back at the temple, Kai was not in a good way. He was a panther, a good teacher, calm and caring but trying to sort this lot out and charge into battle was not something he was good at. But he did as he was told. With the best, he had to work with. Largo ordered them to leave right away along with Jedda. The pair flew high above them as they left the temple and the jungle behind. Kai walked out in front along with Luna and Rajesh. The other elephants, the buffalo, a couple of Nina's other leopard friends but also the slight of gorillas that had managed to get back in time was a big relief to him. They wanted revenge for their home and their family. They told Kai that Blue wasn't coming back just yet but they were there to help in any way they could. The group was small compared to what was out there. They all crossed the river and out into the grassland of the lower valley right in the middle of this mass of men, lions which included left eye and her wolf pack plus many more, it all stretched out for a few miles on route to the capital. None of them could believe just how many they were up against and Kai didn't let them stop for the council. He shouted as they all started to charge straight towards the army of the darkness. Unfortunately, as Marko had predicted, it didn't end well. The fighting didn't even last that long and as much as they tried their hardest, they just couldn't break them down. Most of them just kept going as they were ordered. The elephants tried their hardest to fight and chase down as many as they could. Rajesh was big and stood his ground well, swung his big head and trunk back and forth but the lions got in the way and together with the wolves, they just couldn't run at the men like they wanted to. They all fought. They all knew they were hopelessly outnumbered but they fought anyway. Largo landed with a thud crashing into a big group of men that got the bear's attention as he stopped and looked from up in front where he was. He told everyone to keep moving as he moved back through the group towards the dragon. Largo knew full well he would come straight for him and he was ready to end that bear fight once and for all. Kai and the other leopards were doing well fighting off the wolves and had killed a few men but none of it made any difference. There were too many and Kai knew it. Just then, a flash from above as Yas came in and landed really closer to him.

'Kai,' she shouted, 'pull them back. Pull everyone back.' Kai looked confused.

'What? Why?'

Marko has ordered everyone to Westmoor. Kai smiled. He knew the general was finally awake.

Sahara looked on as the captain and all his men slowly left the small town high up in the mountain heading east of the old fort at Westmoor. Marko and the queen rode together alongside the troops. Sahara was all alone and she felt it she had loved him and wanted him back so much but now he was gone again. They wanted, they needed him to be the general the leader and now she knew that's exactly what he was but that's not what she wanted and she knew it. Alexis and her new little friend slowly crept around the capital. Liv showed her all the short cuts just as she had done with Marko beforehand. They stopped and overheard a group of guards talking about the bear and the army that was on its way. Alexis thought that was not good news for them.

'We can't stay here,' she said to Liv. They carried on a bit further up before reaching the same tunnel that she had taken Marko to.

'In there,' she said. Alexis looked in the dark, wet tunnel.

'What's in there?' she asked.

'The jail.'

'Wait here,' she told her. It was Liv's turn to go in along the dirty, cold water pipe and up into the town's jail. It was indeed full. Every cell but that meant more guards too. The battle was over. Luna and some of the buffalo had gone back over the river. Largo and Yas fought on so the others could get away. None of them saw what was coming until it was too late. Rajesh was working his way back through as much as Luna was in charge. He was a stubborn, old elephant. Whistleroot saw him and knew that'd be a good price for the morning. He ran straight into his blind side and with the full force of the bear's weight knocking the big elephant to his knees. Kai looked on but couldn't reach his friend in time. The two dragons weren't close enough either but Jedda had seen the bear and flew past breathing his fire straight at him. The bear was so angry.

'Come here and fight me,' he shouted out. 'I'll pull your wings off like a dragonfly.' He smiled at the thought of it. Rajesh was winded pretty bad and was struggling to get to his feet but he knew he had to. But no, it was too late. The bear jumped through the fire towards him. He tried desperately. Swung his trunk around but the bear killed him right there and then. Kai, Largo and the others could only watch as the bear killed their friend.

Chapter 13

War Had Begun

It was now late afternoon. Alexis sat outside of a water pipe in the capital waiting for her new friend to come back. Liv had made her way into the jail and had found Mrs French in between a lot of others from the market place and anyone that had been loyal to the queen or the council.

Oh, Liv,' she said to her as she hugged the young girl through the bars. 'What are you doing here?'

'I've come back to save you,' Liv said to her.

'Oh, Liv dear,' the old lady replied to the young girl. 'Where's Marko?' she whispered to her.

'I don't really know,' she said, 'I'm here with May and a couple of others.'

'Oh,' she didn't like the sound of that. 'Look, Liv, listen to me very carefully. You have to go straight back to May and you all have to get out of here. Jasper, the queen's brother, has taken over and they've got their army on its way here right now. Anyone who gets caught will be in trouble. As soon as she said that, Liv knew she wouldn't leave Mrs French in that dark, cold cellar on her own to die. Liv didn't have a choice as the guards were making their rounds.

'Go,' the old woman said to her, 'go back to May. Tell her what I've told you. Get out of the city, Liv, get out,' she said to her, holding her tight. Liv, with tears in her eyes, ducked back down the pipe and out to where Alexis was. Liv was crying by the time she got outside and Alexis gave her a big hug.

'What is it?' she asked. After Liv told her, the two went straight beck to the little house and to where May was. Cassian was also up by the time they got back.

Blue wandered through the forest near to where his home was. The smell of burning and smoke still fill the air. He was lost in his own mind. Confused, he had no idea what he was doing or where he was going. He had lost so much in one go. The humans he lived with were just as part of his family as the gorillas were and there were so many bodies lying around both human and ape alike. The cloudy cover forest of the mountains that Blue called his home felt so empty and he felt completely alone. He walked around for hours not far but just enough. He was hoping, praying he find someone or something or a sound anything but all he got were the birds singing in the late afternoon sun and nothing else. He knew he couldn't stay but he just didn't know where else to go. Blue left his home behind him. He didn't know if he'd ever be back or if any of the others had got away. He walked down through the forest to where it met the foot hills of the upper valley and the middle kingdom.

Marko, Nikita, Marley and Captain Nickolas all finally arrived at the old fort of Westmoor. Soon as they got there, Marko started ordering the captain and all his men around. The queen and the monkey were made safe and comfortable inside and the men went around cleaning the place up and patching it up.

'I want men posted everywhere. Also sweep the whole area for a mile all the way around,' he told them. Marko could barely stand up but Nickolas was impressed by the now general which is what all of the men had started calling him. Inside the old fort were a couple of small bedrooms, a kitchen type looking place and a big hall. The captain and Marko started planning. Marley went up to the tower and just watched out. Nikita even got involved.

'We need number,' Marko said, 'anyone and everyone between the council and the queen, the world needs to see that the light has not left this world. We all know what the darkness is like. They fight each other as much as us, so we stand together stronger.' He was just saying, 'And hope it's enough to scare them off,' when Nickolas interrupted him with a funny look. Marko stopped talking and told him to go. Nikita looked at Marko.

'Funny what was that about?' she asked him.

'I'm not sure there's something funny with him and I can't tell what it is.' The pair carried on talking for a while longer.

Luna and some of the others tried to go back over the river as soon as they saw what had happen to Rajesh but Yas landed right in their way spreading her wings high and wide.

'No,' she shouted, 'you can't go back now. It's too late. We all need to regroup at Westmoor. Luna with tears in her eyes retuned with all the elephants back deep into the jungle and nowhere near where they needed her to be. Kai, the other leopards, gorilla and some of buffalo went north to the old fort. Largo, Yas and Jedda flew high up and watched the army march on. Largo knew what a massive mistake he had made

154

and it was his fault that the bull elephant now lay dead on the battlefield. A couple of hours later, Kai and the others reached the old fort. They were greeted by the men and given water and places to rest. All expect Kai who went straight in and told Marko everything. Marko didn't answer. He just stood there listening when the panther was finished telling him he was told to go rest with the others but Kai had something else to ask first.

'What it is, Kai?'

'Where Nina?' Marko had no idea where she was. He was completely out of it when the twins found May and Nina and by the time, they got back to Thorberg.

He walked over to him and told him, 'I don't know, my friend. Nina and Blue, Harden and the major. They are all missing. May and Alexis and Cassian too.'

'Marko,' Nikita said, 'May and the others are in the capital. I wanted to know what was going on. Sahara wouldn't let them but, in the end, we all agreed that we needed to know. Liv went as well,' she added. The look on his face said it all. She told him that Harden and the dog went to the temple looking for Blue. Kai said that they never showed up.

'Okay,' he said to the pair of them before slowly walking out into the courtyard.

Kane looked on as the men started to arrive and it was then that the news spread of the attack and about the three dragons but also how the bear had killed a bull elephant. Kane couldn't care less what or who that bear kills just as long as it wasn't him. Jasper looked so pleased. 'Look at my new army,' he shouted out from the top of the front gate rubbing his hands together. *The poor boy*, Kane thought to himself, *he has absolutely no idea what his got himself into. He'd be dead by*

the end of the week and I'll by rich and on my way back home.
That brought a smile to his face, but the truth was they were
both being fooled by the same witch. Whistleroot sat on the
battlefield looking on as the last of the men went past south
and on to the capital. The dragons had gone and other animals
then gone. It was only him and the dead which included
Rajesh's body. The bear was evil and nasty with it. He loved
the fighting and proving to everyone that he really wasn't
scared of anything but not this time, he didn't touch the
elephant. He knew Rajesh was a big bull in his prime not only
was it disrespectful to eat him, it was his way of sending
everyone else a message.

'There's no time to lose,' Cassian said to them, 'we get out
of here right now. With an army coming, we'd get trapped in
here.' May thought for a minute. She told the twins to go and
get the horses ready. She needed to do something first. They
left without saying a word.

'Liv,' she said, 'show me the quickest way down to the
harbour.' Within minutes, the pair were down by the docks but
this time, she couldn't see what it was that she was looking
for. *Where is he*, she thought to herself, *damn that man*. But
then, she caught sight of it. It wasn't the man she was looking
for rather the boat itself.

'See there.' She pointed. 'That's the boat.' Liv looked
over.

'Yes, I can see it,' she said.

'Do you think you can swim that far?' The boat wasn't out
in the deep water but is wasn't in the harbour either. She didn't
look very sure but she still said yes.

'Very bravely good girl,' May said to her. 'Take this.' She
gave the little girl the bit of string that the master gave to her.

'Swim out to the boat and ask for Captain Tai. Show him this and tell him May-li sent you. May whispered the rest of her plan to Liv before watching the girl get in the water and swim off. She waiting a couple more minutes before leaving her hoping and praying that Tai would get the message. Cassian and his sister were all ready and waiting in the stable.

'Where is she?' he said to Alexis.

'Stop worrying,' she said back to him, 'she'll be here. We trusted her once, there's no reason not to do that now.' A few more minutes passed and just as Cassian was about to moan about where she was, May rushed back in.

'Oh, thank God you're safe,' he said to her.

'Where's the little girl?' Alexis asked her.

'She's safe. Now let's get out of here.'

Sahara ordered her bodyguards to ready her carriage. The hasky dogs that pulled it were ready for a run out. She left her study and went up to her room. There she changed out of her gorgeous dress she had been wearing into something a bit more suited for battle. Her white, elegant dress had given way to black leather boots, brown trousers, white blouse and a dark corset. Her hair was tied back with her arm guards on. She had her sword in one hand and her wand in the other. She knew the time had come for her and Marko to finally finish this battle and after that, finally share the love that they felt for each other. She might not have like him for what he had become but he was like that before. After the fight was over, she knew he and her would finally be together in love. Within hours, she had left Thorberg behind and was on her way to Westmoor on her way to Marko.

Sasha was still in her castle. She too was getting ready to leave. She didn't have a carriage like Sahara did. Instead she rode a big, black horse called Luca. She didn't have a sword or any reason to get changed or ready because she had been ready and for a long time. Her plan was in full swing. All the pieces to her puzzle were exactly where they needed to be. The people she picked had done everything that she had asked of them. The master dead, Blue's home destroyed, the council weakened by her and their army. She laughed to herself HAHAHA what army and before they had either known it too, but she didn't trust one single one of them and of course planned to kill them all in the end. The council, Kane, the bear, they were all the same in her eyes but just not yet. She just had to hold on a little longer. She wasn't in the capital just yet and the kingdom wasn't her either, plus she knew the same as everyone else that she too was on the bear's menu if she wasn't too careful.

She tried very hard to keep calm and keep her temper under control. It was her biggest downfall and she knew that as long as everything was going her way, she knew she'd be queen of the whole world soon enough and a queen of darkness at that.

To be continued.